WALK ON

AMY McLEAN

Copyright © 2013 Amy McLean

All rights reserved.

ISBN: 1491201908
ISBN-13: 978-1491201909

First edition published in 2013
Second edition published in 2014

For Auntie Elsie

The ground beneath me buries itself into the backs of my legs. It forces itself against me: cold, concrete, uneven. It begins to numb right through me until I am no longer able to feel anything. I move a hand down towards the hard surface, wincing a protest of disgust as it collides with the soil. Dry clumps of mud litter the dirty surface. I press my back against the wall behind me in an attempt to feel its support. As I arrange myself in an attempt to beat the discomfort, chalky flakes of the brickwork behind me crumble and fall down; it mixes with the dust that lines the floor, forming a grubby blanket.

I struggle to breathe properly as I inhale the thick air. I can taste the grainy substance with each breath, smothering my lungs with its tiny, intrusive particles. I shiver as the bitterness of the draft circles around me, enveloping me in a chill. I don't know where it is coming from. I pull my knees closer into my chest so that I'm curled upright in a ball; my arms wrap around my legs tightly to try and generate a little of my own warmth.

Leaning forward, I rest my forehead on my knees. I decide that this is the safest way to sit; I don't know what lies in front of me; I can't begin to imagine what might sit beside me. In the darkness I'm unable to see even my hand as I hold it up in front of me.

But this is the way I like it. In this blackness, nobody can find me. Nobody can see where I am. I have no desire to move outside of my four walls. They keep me secure, protected from the outside world. I may not be able to find a way out, but he can't get in either. He cannot harm me in here.

Not a single thread of contamination from the world outside is able to weave its way into my walls. There is no window for anybody to peer through. Nothing cannot disturb my loneliness. No door exists for anybody to cross through. I long to progress deeper into my walls, further inside so I can explore where I know it will be free of soil and dirt and mud and dust. I'm certain that there's a section where beautiful, natural light still exists. The air is warm and pure there, not heavy and cold like it is here.

If I could find a way to see through the darkness, I would be able to make my way to that part of my four walls, the part that will free me from my internal pain. It would release the ache in my heart, the constant torture in my mind. But still, I know he cannot hurt me while I am in here. Nobody can touch me for as long as I remain within my four walls.

book. Josie had moved down to England when she landed a job with one of London's local newspapers a few years ago. To ensure they remained in touch they would often send little treats to each other in the post, but it seemed to Maggie that a book was a most peculiar gift. Josie hadn't even mentioned that she was sending anything when they spoke on the phone the previous week.

Maggie had looked over the book briefly when she slipped it out of the envelope, unsure of what to expect. She had heard of Mary Wollstonecraft, she was fairly certain, though she knew very little about her.

She decided she might as well give the book a try. She had nothing to lose, and it was the least she could do since Josie had gone to the trouble of posting it out to her. She buttoned up her jacket and wrapped her stripy purple scarf around her neck, before sliding *A Vindication of the Rights of Woman* into her bag.

As she was sitting on the wooden bench reading the book, she found herself becoming absorbed in the text. She became fascinated by what the writer was suggesting. Before long, Maggie had begun to develop an emotional connection with the words. Each page seemed to speak to her in ways she couldn't have imagined, but she couldn't quite put her finger on why this was. She was just about to begin a new chapter when, out of the corner of her eye, she noticed something float down from the tree that stood directly above her.

Lying peacefully on the seat beside her was the little leaf. It was curled over, tucked within itself as if sleeping. Maggie couldn't help but admire its natural beauty as she picked it up by its small stalk and twisted it around in her fingers. The gentle breeze tickled the leaf as she held it. She placed her bookmark, which she had fashioned out of the note from her sister that came with the gift, into the book and closed it, turning her full attention to the leaf. She sat for a moment, studying its delicate edges as she gently stretched it out. She loved the way each vein seemed to reach out hungrily from its center. The vision came to her straight away for a new scrapbook page; she knew exactly what she wanted to do with this little leaf.

Maggie had been working on this particular piece all afternoon. She'd managed to dig out a loose sheet of burnt orange coloured card from the stash in her cupboard, and immediately proceeded to create a decorative border for the display. She had decided to create something colourful and fun, using images from a sheet of dainty Halloween-themed stickers: white ghosts that promised to glow in the dark; tiny broomsticks with bright orange tails; black cats with yellow eyes luminous. The vibrant colours would help frame the more natural shades of the scene in the middle, she decided.

The rest of the card she decorated with a variety of seasonal symbols. Using articles from an old box of artist pencils, she sketched out the silhouette of a tree, allowing it to grow and stretch right up the side of the page. She shaded it in a dark grey before drawing a small cluster of apples at its base, some of which she coloured red, and the rest green. She took care in drawing each one with precision, ensuring that each was similar in size to the rest. Satisfied with the fruit, she moved on to work with the main attraction of the page.

Maggie had used a tiny amount of PVC glue to stick her leaf the page, dabbing a little in the center and at each of its corners. It hadn't dried too well, however, so she ended up having to fashion a leaf shape out of a sheet of sticky-back plastic, which she then gently placed on top of the leaf. As she pressed out the air bubbles the leaf let out a little crackling sound, as if announcing that it was starting to dry out, losing the last of its breath. Once she was finished securing it down, Maggie couldn't help but gaze at how much at rest the leaf looked, without a care in the world. She sat back and admired the finished piece.

Reaching towards a selection of pens that sat inside an old plastic cup, she pulled out a black fineliner. She had left just enough space to the left side of the pumpkin for her to sign her name. She curved the *M* of her forename, before finishing with *Fallon* in her swirly handwriting. She concluded the last letter with an assertive flick.

Snapping her attention back to the reality around her, she turned to the clock. Maggie realised that she only had ten minutes left before Peter was due to arrive home from work. Hastily, she shoveled all of her craft supplies into the large crate she used to store her materials in, and dragged it hurriedly into the cupboard in the hallway.

Not wanting to risk putting away her scrapbook just yet in case the glue still needed time to dry, she slid it onto the top of the bookshelf in the living room, out of the way of the table. She looked around her quickly to make sure she'd not left anything out before advancing to the kitchen.

"Oh, hurry up. Come on!" She complained to

the taps as they trickled hot water into the sink basin. Squirting the washing up liquid into the water, she swished it around, before plunging the morning's breakfast dishes into it. "I knew I should have done them before I sat down with the scrapbook," she sighed to herself. She'd been too excited though to think of anything else.

Frantically, she scrubbed the little lumps of congealed strawberry jam off of the surface of the plates, washing away the little flecks of toast crumbs. Making sure there were no rings of coffee stains inside the mugs, she wiped at them with a sponge to clean them up.

After emptying the basin out and rinsing the dishes of their suds, she finished drying the crockery, before crashing them back into the cupboard as she rushed to tidy them away. She knew better than to have dirty dishes lying around when Peter arrived home from work. She couldn't let him know that she'd been sitting around all day working on her art.

Maggie's mobile phone bleeped as she placed the last of the plates away. As she dried her hands on the tea towel, she walked back into the living room to retrieve her phone from where she'd left it on the table. It flashed up a text message from Lucy: *Hi Maggie, Just making sure everything is still okay for this evening? Looking forward to it! Lucy xx* Maggie typed in a response and hit 'send'. The phone took a few seconds to acknowledge that she was trying to send a reply; she'd been using the same phone for five years, and the battery was starting to struggle to cooperate. She refused to even look into buying a new mobile though until it was a case of not having any other choice. Lucy had praised her own new phone just the week before, and had tried to persuade Maggie to try out one of the latest models on the market, but Maggie wasn't interested. She didn't see the need for "all these fancy smart-thingys, with their grubby touch-screens and weird apps and Angry Pigs, or whatever they're called," she had protested. She much preferred the more natural delights of life; technology was something she had never really been able to get along with.

She placed her phone back on the table and looked up. As she did so, she noticed a white feather that was sat in the center of the table. It must have escaped from the crafts box, she thought as she stared at it. For some reason, she found herself transfixed, unable to move or take her eyes away from the feather.

"I'm sure I didn't miss anything," she mumbled to herself as she was finally able to pick up the feather. As she held it in her hand, she tried to remember when she would have purchased it, but struggled to remember ever having a need to buy a pack of feathers.

There was something oddly attractive about this particular feather. It couldn't have been any greater than five inches in length, but as it curved upwards from the palm of Maggie's hand, it appeared to be so grand and powerful, as if it were reaching up to the sky. Maggie had never felt anything as soft as the feather before. She brushed her finger along the edge, allowing the tiny fibers to stroke her skin with a comforting warmth.

The feather was the brightest, purest white she had ever seen. Not a single blemish could be found on its surface. As she moved it over, Maggie was sure it was almost sparkling at her. It seemed to have a faint silvery shimmer to it, glistening as it caught the light. Maggie had become almost mesmerised by its beauty, and wondered why she couldn't remember buying it.

Suddenly aware of the time again, she headed back into the hallway, and placed the feather into the crate in the cupboard with the rest of the supplies. As the clock in the living room announced that it was now six o'clock, she went back into the kitchen and filled the kettle with water, before turning it on to boil. She set two cups on the side of the counter, and spooned the coffee granules into the bottom of each.

The front door opened, before closing shut with a heavy hand. "Peter?" Maggie called out as she began to pour the hot water into the mugs.

Peter didn't bother to respond as he clumped through the hallway, his boots heavy against the wooden floor. As he walked into the living room, he took his jacket off and flung it up onto the door before slouching himself down on the sofa.

"Good day?" Maggie asked from the kitchen, having turned to acknowledge Peter's arrival. The spoon clinked against the mugs as she stirred the drinks.

Peter rested back against the sofa. "It wasn't bad. Some idiot customer tried to get a refund on a packet of biscuits that they'd already opened. I just thought to myself, 'It's not my fault if you thought they were chocolate creams, love! Read the label next time.' What's worse is that she'd already eaten half the packet! I mean, how many vanilla creams do you need to eat before you realise that there's no chocolate in them? What an idiot!"

Maggie smiled, amused. "Here you go," she responded as she carried the two mugs of coffee through into the living room, and handed the blue one to Peter.

He sat up as he stretched for the mug. "Thanks. And this," he reached into his trouser pocket, "is for you." He handed the white envelope to Maggie.

"What is it?" She sat down in the chair beside the bookshelf, placing her mug on a coaster next to her.

"I've no idea. It was sticking out of the letter box. Addressed to you: *Mrs Maggie Gordon.*" Peter enunciated her name.

"I must have missed it when the postman came this morning." She tore open the back of the envelope and pulled out the sheet of paper from the inside. She sighed, disappointed at the anti-climax. "Oh. How exciting. More junk mail. We don't need a new lawn mower, do we? I don't even know how they know the addresses to send these things to."

"Oh, I've no clue. People can get hold of all sorts of information these days." Peter blew on the surface of the hot liquid before taking a sip of coffee. "I do wish you'd stop using that name though."

"It's my name, Peter." Maggie stuffed the paper back into the envelope and dropped it onto the bookshelf. She picked up her own mug and cradled the warmth.

"You know I hate it though. It just sounds so… common! 'Oh, Maggie! *Maggie!*'" he mocked, throwing his voice so that it squeaked at her. "You might as well stand on a street corner wearing plastic boots and fishnets and be done with it."

"I'm pretty sure you're over-reacting, Peter. Besides, everybody calls me Maggie. They always have. Even the teachers at school knew me as Maggie." Her mobile phone bleeped again. Maggie leaned forward to reach for it from the table. She read the text message that had popped up on the screen, before delivering it to Peter. "Lucy says we have to meet them at the restaurant at seven."

Peter sighed. "Do we *have* to go? Will it really make a difference if we just don't turn up?"

"Yes, Peter. We have to go. It's her fortieth birthday. All she's asking for is an intimate meal, just the four of us. I'm sure you can manage that."

"I don't see what the big deal is. I mean, forty. It's just a number. I've been forty for several years now, and I still don't feel any different."

"Well," Maggie started, "it's an important age for some people. After all, they do say life begins at…"

"When you turned forty, you spent all day complaining and moping!" Peter interrupted. "You kept whining that time was moving too fast, and that you didn't want to get old. I'm not sure how that brings any reason to celebrate. The only reason birthdays exist is to remind us that we're constantly moving faster towards death."

Maggie ran her finger along the side of the bookshelf next to her. "Well, yes. I admit that I probably could have handled my own fortieth better. But Lucy wants to celebrate her birthday, so we're going to do as she asks. It's just a meal she's asking for. She won't make you do anything crazy, you know."

"It's not Lucy that bothers me. It's that…Graham, or George, or…"

"Gary."

"Yes, Gary. Whatever. He just goes on and on

about his stupid fish tank. How many guppies can one man need?" Peter drained the last of his coffee and stood up.

"He's not that bad. Besides, we'll only be there a few hours. And I hear it's not a bad restaurant apparently."

Peter took his mug into the kitchen and placed it on the counter. "What's the name of this 'not a bad restaurant'?"

Maggie followed him into the kitchen. "I can't remember, actually. I should really have written it down."

"Sounds good, then."

"It's just down from Union Street, though. I don't think it's anything too fancy, just traditional British food I believe."

"Is it the one that's inside the hotel?"

"I think it might be, yes." Despite the fact that they'd both lived in Aberdeen all of their life, neither of them seemed to take advantage of the social offerings. If they ate out at a restaurant that didn't have a drive-thru, it was only because Maggie had insisted that they had to attend somebody's function or birthday party. Since they were rarely given the opportunity to go out anywhere, Peter wasn't really in a position to complain too much about it. That didn't stop him though.

Peter rolled his eyes. "I bet it's expensive."

"Let's try and not worry about the cost. I know Lucy can sometimes have rather pricey taste, but…"

"Sometimes?! That woman's doesn't know when to stop spending! I swear Gary just hands everything to her, the fool. I'd be surprised if they would even be willing to pay less than three figures for a tin of beans."

"...but I don't think it'll be that bad." Maggie finished. "Worst case scenario, we skip the starters, and go straight for the main course."

Peter sighed. "Right then, seeing as it seems that I don't exactly have a choice in the matter, I suppose I better go and get ready. Here," he moved his mug into the basin. "You do the dishes and I'll go and take a shower."

Maggie stared at the bottle of washing up liquid as Peter walked out of the room. Rolling up her sleeves, she began filling up the basin with water once again, a chore she was all too familiar with. She felt as though her life consisted of nothing more than housework, and Maggie knew there was nothing she could do about it.

When she was a little girl, Maggie used to spend hours sitting at her desk with her sketch book proudly displayed in front of her. Every evening after she had finished her homework – and sometimes before she had even started it if she could get away with it – she would take care over sharpening all of her pencils and arranging them like the colours of a beautiful rainbow. In her youth, she would often work on drawings inspired by the works of her favourite artists. Above her desk she used to hang a reprint of Claude Monet's 'Bridge over a Pool of Water Lilies'. The little framed image had moved around with Maggie ever since, and it currently found itself hanging on her bedroom wall where she knew she would be able to look at it every morning before starting the day.

As she grew up, she found that she was constantly designing pictures and scenes that focused on a bridge as its central image. She was fascinated by the way they curved or stretched across the land, appearing unsupported and yet stable. The flowing water beneath always looked so cool and calming. What it must be like to be a tiny little water lily swaying down the stream! She'd think to herself. She found the tranquility of the pictures to be incredibly soothing and peaceful.

Her bridges were usually created without any people walking over them, as she found that she preferred her scenes to focus entirely on nature without the corruption of human life invading it. However, there was one occasion where she had found herself sketching somebody - or something - standing in the center of the bridge.

The night before, she had dreamed the image in her head. When she awoke in the morning she could still see it as clearly in her mind as she had in her sleep. Something told her that she needed to replicate the vision onto the blank page of her sketchpad that sat open at her desk, waiting for her.

She began working on the bridge first in the center of the page, taking her time to make sure that it reached across the paper with enough room for her to add in the river below. She shaped the grassy banks at either side of the water, and added in the outlines for what would later become narrow, bare trees all over the moss-green banks.

She observed the page, recognising that, at this stage, it looked just like many of her other bridge paintings. Except with this one, she knew she wasn't ready to begin adding any colour to it. She still had a job to do.

She found that her sketch of the figure in her

dream almost poured right out of her hand. The image was imprinted in her mind; it took little effort for her to recall and focus on it. The vision seemed so natural, so detailed.

Maggie gave her the golden brown curls that had cascaded softly down over her shoulders in the dream. She wore a beautiful dress that flowed right down to her ankles, coloured at first glance in a delicate ivory, but upon closer inspection it offered a tint of soft blue.

Once she had finished drawing the scene and had added the colour, she looked at her design. Something was missing. Maggie knew that this woman was the most beautiful being she had ever seen. Her eyes were wide, each one a watery bright blue. Her skin was pale and delicate. She looked wonderful. But something wasn't quite right.

Taking her pencil, Maggie found herself drawing two arches, each one appearing as if it was growing right out of the woman's shoulders. She realised after a minute that she was sketching a set of wings. They stretched right down to the waist, large and powerful, flowing with elegance in the invisible breeze.

Once she was finished drawing the wings, she studied the figure's appearance thoughtfully. Is she a fairy? She wondered to herself. She certainly seemed to resemble a fairy, with her dainty little features and delicate wings. Each one seemed to be made up of little sections, but Maggie couldn't quite work out what they were. She decided to leave the wings as they were without any colour; for some reason, she couldn't remember if the wings had even had any colour to them in her dream. It was the one part of her vision to which she had been allowed little access.

Maggie looked at her drawing from all angles, making sure she hadn't left anything out. Upon doing so, she decided that this was the finest piece of artwork she had ever produced. She was, of course, proud of lots of her other drawings, and loved to display her paintings around the house, but there was something different about this one. Something special. She didn't want to share it with anybody else. No, the woman with the wings was to be reserved for Maggie's eyes only. She took care in punching two little holes into the side of the picture, and, reaching over to her fluffy teddy bear that always sat on the side of her desk, keeping Maggie company while she worked, she began untying the silver ribbon from around the toy's snowy white neck. After threading this through the holes in the picture of the winged woman, Maggie tied it neatly into a little bow. She placed the picture in her top drawer, burying it beneath the layers of thick jumpers and pyjamas to keep it safe. Yes, she decided, she liked that picture very much.

She was sure that it was in her destiny to become a successful artist. She would grow up to paint portraits of sophisticated businessmen, and sketch images of cats basking lazily in the hot sun. Or maybe she'd become an illustrator for children's books. Josie was forever scribbling down stories and filling countless notebooks, and Maggie would often sketch out ideas and designs for book covers to accompany her sister's writing. They'd make a great team, she was sure.

Instead of painting portraits or shading in cartoon characters, Maggie stood in front of the kitchen sink with her hands plunged into the hot water, the soapy bubbles creeping up towards her elbows as she washed the last mug. She gazed out of the window and looked out into the shared garden. Her upstairs neighbour's Staffordshire Bull Terrier was wandering round, sniffing the fence that surrounded the grass. Maggie wondered if she'd ever get a dog. "I reckon it'd have to be a large dog, like an Alsatian, or a Great Dane," she voiced, not realising she was speaking out loud. "It's not as if I wouldn't have the time to look after a dog. If nothing else, I would rather appreciate the company during the daytime. Perhaps a Dalmatian would be nice." She sighed, and picked up the tea towel to dry the dishes once more.

"I'm just saying, Margaret, it wouldn't be my first choice!" Peter walked towards the restaurant door. Maggie followed a step behind him, clutching onto a gift bag.

"I'm pretty sure that there are few people in the world who choose where they celebrate their birthday based on the size of the car park, Peter."

He stopped outside the door. "I'm sure it wouldn't have hurt to give it a thought. I mean, I would have had to park right out on the street if it wasn't for that jeep pulling out just as we were arriving." He gestured to the door. "After you!"

Maggie opened it and walked inside, Peter entering reluctantly after her. "Well this is huge…"

Maggie nudged Peter to stop his sarcasm. They spotted Lucy and Gary in the corner. "It's fine, Peter. I'm sure there are smaller restaurants," Maggie uttered under her breath. "Plus, we've never been in here before, so you can think of it as a new experience."

"Every cloud."

"Maggie!" Lucy jumped up from her seat as soon as she saw her best friend approaching the table. She greeted her, squeezing Maggie tightly.

"How many have you had?!" Maggie laughed, as she eased Lucy's energy away from her and handed her the gift bag inside which she'd stored Lucy's birthday present.

"I've not actually had a drink yet! I'm just happy to see you, silly. Ooh, a present!" Lucy's eyes lit up as she spoke with excitement. She turned to Peter with a smile. "Hello, Peter."

"Happy birthday, Lucy. Gary." Peter nodded and sat down at the table opposite Gary. The two women carried on chatting as they remained standing at the end of the table to catch up.

"How's the job going, Peter?" Gary peered through his glasses at the menu in front of him, not looking up at Peter as he spoke.

"It's not bad," Peter replied, relieved for a chance to talk about his own interests instead of having to listen to Gary's monotonous tales. "It's been six months now since I received my promotion. It's keeping me on my toes, so it is, but I wouldn't have it any other way."

"That must be nice for you." He still didn't look up as he spoke, his words lacking enthusiasm. They sat in silence for a moment, before Gary suddenly set his menu down and turned his full attention towards Peter. "Did you know that Oscar fish love their food? Oh, they are such greedy little devils! You know, Peter, I bought the most beautiful wee Oscar from that pet shop down by the beach, you know the one with all the rabbits and hamsters and stuff? They have quite a selection in there! Anyway, he was the most adorable little thing, all black but with these delicate little orange markings all over his front. I decided to name him Wilde. Well, I put Wilde in the tank, and he was darting around, all merry and playful. He ate his pellets, just like all the other fish. Good Wilde, I told him. You're a very clever boy for eating up your food. But I must have jinxed it! Do you know what he did?"

"What?"

"He only decided to eat the other fish!"

"Is that so?" Peter gazed his eyes over the menu as a distraction from yet another one of Gary's dull fish stories. He should have known there would have been no escape.

"Yes! When I came down the next morning, the Neon Tetras had all disappeared. Wilde had battered the Guppies, and Fluffy didn't look too impressed either. Fluffy is Lucy's catfish…"

"Oh, Gary, no fish talk tonight, please!" Lucy spoke as she turned to sit back down at the table. Maggie slid into the seat next to Peter.

"I was only telling Peter about how Wilde ate the other…"

"Oh, look, they have food!" Maggie grinned as Lucy interrupted her husband; she didn't think she'd be able to suffer another fish story either. She wondered how Lucy coped with them every day. Lucy turned her own attention to the choices in front of her. "It all looks amazing. I don't know what to have!"

"I think I'm not going to bother with a starter."

"You're not on a diet are you, Maggie? You hardly need to trim down! And you look amazing in that dress." Lucy offered her friend reassurance, speaking truthfully. She was aware of Maggie's insecurities about her appearance; even at school, Maggie never seemed to possess the greatest of confidence. "Actually, isn't that the really expensive one that was in the window of Debenhams last week? It's gorgeous!"

Maggie panicked. "What, this old thing? No, no. Not at all! I just plucked it out the back of my wardrobe this afternoon. I've had it for years, but never had the chance to wear it," Maggie lied. A few weeks ago, she and Lucy had decided to meet in town to go for a coffee. Just as it was usually the case with Lucy, the morning led to an afternoon of shopping, or, in Maggie's case, browsing. As soon as Maggie had approached the window of the department store, her eyes lit up. The dress was being modeled by a mannequin. There was something mesmerising about the way the sleek design hung loosely onto the model's petite frame.

It was the vibrant purple colour that lured her closer. As she approached the dress, she realised that it was impossible for her to not fall in love with its dainty little straps. The delicate horizontal ruching that filled the front of the garment adhered exactly to her tastes. She knew she couldn't possibly condone buying it, she told herself. Peter would never allow it. She knew she had to forget about the dress. But she couldn't.

On a whim she found herself taking a detour from her usual walk the following day as she headed straight into town and directly to the changing rooms of the shop, clutching the dress in her hands.

She knew it was a big mistake. As soon as she

had slipped the dress over her head, she couldn't help but love with the way the gentle tailoring shaped her hips. It didn't sit on her the way it did on the mannequin, but she decided that it worked very well with her natural curves; she was normally very self-conscious about her shape, but the luscious purple seemed to detract from her least favourite aspects of herself, and the colour was a good match for her own pale complexion.

She knew she shouldn't have bought it. It was far too expensive. She had panicked, had tried to find the receipt to take it back. It was nowhere to be seen. She would have to keep the dress and pray that Peter didn't notice anything. She was sure he never paid attention to what she wore. It would be fine. She hoped.

"Oh, well it's very beautiful!" Lucy replied.

"Yes, it's an interesting dress, Margaret. Don't you think it's a bit low-cut, though?" Peter questioned.

"Don't be daft, Peter! There's no such thing as too low-cut!" Lucy answered on behalf of Maggie, whose cheeks had begun to turn a dark shade of pink. Lucy's own dress plunged at the neck, with an equally low scoop down its back.

"Are you ready to order?" The waitress approached the table without warning, carrying a notepad and pen in her hands, calling a halt to the conversation. Maggie breathed, relieved.

"I think I'll go for the Chicken Highlander, and, to drink, I think...yes, let's get a bottle of dry white wine for the table, if everybody's happy with that?" Gary asked. The party nodded in unison.

The waitress turned to Lucy. "And for you,

madam?"

"Could I have the Haddock and Prawn Mornay, please?"

"Certainly." She scribbled the order down on the notepad.

"And I'll have the cheddar macaroni and cheese, thanks." Peter added.

Maggie paused for a second while the waitress asked for her order. She had studied all of the prices, hoping that something inexpensive would catch her attention. She finally ordered, "I'll just have the smoked Scottish salmon please, and a glass of water, thanks." She sighed when she saw that Peter hadn't noticed that she'd made the effort to choose the cheapest meal on the menu. She was still worrying about the dress.

"You not having a proper drink, Maggie?"

"She can't, can she?" Peter responded on behalf of his wife. "Somebody's got to be able to drive the car home, and after the day I've had at work, I think I deserve a drink!"

The waitress interjected, "If that's everything, I shall send your order through to the kitchen for you."

"Yes, thank you." Lucy replied. The waitress walked off and disappeared towards the back of the room. "Goodness, I'm starving! The smell of the food coming from the other table is almost making me drool!" She tried not to inhale the whiff of gravy that was drifting towards her.

"It's really lovely in here, Lucy," Maggie announced as she took in the atmosphere. "The crimson goes really well with the dark wood."

"I think the décor's one of the reasons I chose it, actually. When I first came here – it would have been about two years ago now, I imagine – they had the most beautiful red candles on the table in little gold coloured dishes. It was so romantic! We've been here quite a few times since then. Haven't we, Gary?"

"What? Oh, yes. Quite a few times." Gary spluttered a cough.

The waitress returned to the table and placed Maggie's glass of water to the side of her cutlery. She turned towards Gary. "Your wine, sir."

The bottle was presented at the table, and the three glasses were shared out accordingly. Gary proceeded to pour out the drinks before raising his own glass. "A toast, to my beautiful wife. You may be forty, Lucy, but you don't look a day over thirty-nine!"

Peter rolled his eyes. How many times had he heard that one?

"Oh, thank you, Gary! That's really sweet." Lucy blushed slightly, her cheeks matching the colour of her lipstick. "And thank you Maggie, and you too Peter, for joining us this evening to help us celebrate!" Lucy took a sip from her own glass. "Wow, forty! They say that this is the age when life begins, don't they? I've got to say, I've been very lucky so far! I'm not really sure I'd be able to handle it if things improved any more!"

Lucy always seemed to have good luck on her side. As far as Maggie could tell, she was happily married. Her four-bedroom home with the large garden and patio was certainly something worthy of boasting about. She went from strength to strength at work. She had left school with fewer qualifications than Maggie, but landed a job almost instantly as a supervisor in a little café. Not long after she was promoted to the position of the café's manager, she decided to open up her own bakery, and now she specialised in selling cupcakes. Maggie wasn't sure how she'd done it. She wasn't jealous of her friend, but Lucy's endless success did force Maggie to feel even smaller than she already did. She couldn't let it show though.

Maggie smiled across the table. "That's wonderful, Lucy, it really is. I always told you that you'd have nothing to worry about."

"I know, I know. I was just a huge worrier back in school. I was so thankful when Mrs Marten allocated you to be my buddy in second year. I was terrified about moving schools! I don't know how I would have settled in without you."

"I'm sure you would have managed! But I'm glad that she put us together, Lucy. I remember I needed a partner for the art project, but everybody else had already been paired up. Mind, I don't know how much use you were; your little clay horse turned out to be slightly on the wonky side!" Maggie teased.

"I know. I felt terrible. I wondered why he wasn't standing up on his own! I mean, who bakes a clay horse with a missing leg?!" Lucy suddenly remembered her present. "Ooh, let's have a look at what's in here!" She reached for the gift bag that she'd set down by the side of her chair, and pulled at the red ribbon that Maggie had tied around the handle. She'd filled the inside with dark red pieces of confetti, each one displaying either 'Happy Birthday' or '40' in swirly lettering.

From inside the bag, Lucy pulled out a square white box, upon which squiggly silver writing sprawled across branding the illegible name of a jeweller's. Lucy opened up the box carefully. "Oh wow, Maggie!"

Gary leaned over towards Lucy to see what was inside the box. "Fancy!"

"Oh, Maggie. They're absolutely beautiful. They really are!" Lucy exclaimed.

"What did we buy her?" Peter asked, only half interested.

Lucy turned the gift box around away from her. "Aren't they amazing? I'm very spoilt! Thank you, Maggie. Thank you, Peter."

"Yes, you're, welcome, Lucy." Peter's eyes widened when he saw the earrings.

"You women and your jewellery! This one has drawers full of the stuff at home. I don't know how she ever expects to wear it all, yet she swears that she still needs more!"

"You can never have too much jewellery, Gary. That's crazy talk." She placed the box back into the little gift bag, and smiled across the table. "Really, Maggie, they're wonderful. They must have cost you a fortune!"

"Yes, Margaret, how much *did* they cost?"

"She can't answer that, Peter!" Gary spluttered as he sipped the wine.

Peter darted his eyes at Maggie as she held onto her glass, nervously running her fingers around the top of it with her other hand. Peter couldn't get the image of the studs out of his mind. He had no idea what they were, or what the stone was meant to be. He didn't care. All he knew was that the blue jewels that sat in the middle of those little silver flowers would definitely not have been cheap. He could feel his wallet pulsing in his back pocket as he recalled the way the light bounced from the edges of the earrings. He forced the pound-coin sized beads of sweat back into his throbbing veins. Maggie avoided Peter's gaze as she watched him drain his glass and reach for the bottle of wine.

Chapter Two

Maggie waved out of the car window as Lucy and Gary walked off round the corner. They had decided to go for a walk down to the beach; the evening wind had turned surprisingly warm for November, so Lucy had suggested that they take a stroll. Peter had announced that he wasn't in the mood though. Lucy did try to persuade him to change his mind, but Maggie had encouraged them to go alone so as to not risk Peter's anger.

"The lighting in there has given me the worst headache," Peter complained as he fiddled with the glove box. "Do you think we can sue them? I bet we could." Maggie didn't mention the fact that it was more plausible that it was the million glasses of wine Peter had drained that was the cause of his sore head. She clicked her seatbelt into place and slid the car key into the ignition.

"I'm sure you could," she responded dryly. She was too tired to disagree with him.

"And that macaroni and cheese was a waste of time," Peter continued with his complaint. "I can still feel it sticking in my throat." Peter lifted his hand up to scratch his neck. Maggie had actually enjoyed her meal, or what there was of her tiny portion, but she kept quiet, ignoring Peter's remark. "Gary's food didn't look too bad, mind. At least it smelled okay from where I was sitting. Did you see the price of it though? Who pays that much for a bit of chicken?! We sell whole chickens for a quarter of the price at work. What a rip-off!"

"You seemed to enjoy the wine though." Maggie spoke, concentrating on the road as she pulled out of the car park. She was hoping she could find a way to lighten Peter's mood.

"Ah yes, I must admit that the wine was very good. I suspect it probably shouldn't have been the highlight of the entire evening, but I can't complain too much. At least there are no more birthdays you consider important now. It's all downhill from here."

"It won't be too long until your fiftieth..."

"As I said, no more important birthdays," Peter interrupted. "Look at that idiot in the blue Twingo." He pointed an accusing finger at the car two places in front of them on the road. "Learn to drive in the right lane, you moron!" He shouted pointlessly to the Renault, whose right tires had crossed onto the other side of the road.

Maggie carried on down South College Street as the traffic lights turned back to green. She peered into the rear view mirror, and noticed that the back seats were littered with bits of paper and an old cardboard box from a take-away. She only ever drove the car when Peter needed a chauffeur; it was his car, as he kept reminding her. "What a pig," she mumbled to herself as she averted her attention from the mess.

"What?"

"Oh, I was just reminding myself that I need to buy hoover bags tomorrow," she replied, impressing herself at the speed of her ability to come up with a cover.

"Good idea. I noticed the hallway needed cleaning today, and I imagine the bedroom probably needs going over too. You might as well do the whole flat tomorrow while you're at it."

Maggie sighed as she pulled the car up to the next set of traffic lights. She watched as an elderly couple walked hand in hand across the road. "Isn't that sweet?"

"Take me to Asda." Peter ignored her comment. "I want more wine."

Maggie hesitated before responding. The last thing she wanted Peter to consume was more wine. He'd already had more than enough for his level of tolerance this evening. However, she knew better than to refuse his requests, especially when he'd been drinking.

"Are you sure, Peter? I imagine it'll be quite busy at this time in the evening."

"Positive."

He didn't say anything else for the rest of the journey as Maggie detoured along a side street and continued along the dual carriageway. As he sat in silence, Maggie wondered what was going through his mind. She knew he had always liked a drink, but lately he seemed to be consuming alcohol in much larger quantities. She couldn't really work out why, and was always too scared to ask him.

"Are you coming in?" she asked as she unfastened her seatbelt. She had managed to park the car near the entrance of the shop. Thankfully, it didn't seem to be as busy as she had anticipated.

"No, I'll wait. Leave the engine running so I can listen to the radio." He jabbed his finger onto the button to sound the radio. He flicked through the stations at speed until he found one that was playing some jazz song. He wasn't sure what it was, but he began nodding along to the rhythm.

Maggie reached for her bag before opening the car door. "I won't be long." She stepped out into the fresh air, shutting the door behind her.

She hurried across the car park and walked into the entrance of the shop. The warm breeze that was shooting out of the overhead heater in the doorway welcomed her in. She never understood why they had those right in the entrance; it was lovely to walk into, but when leaving the shop the sudden blast of warmth just seemed like a punishment for leaving to go back out into the cold.

Her heels clicked on the solid floor as she headed down the aisles to make her way towards the rows of alcoholic beverages. Had Peter specified what type of wine he'd wanted? She couldn't remember. She glanced at the shelves and grabbed a bottle, hoping it would be enough to keep him happy.

As she carried the bottle to the checkout, she couldn't help but take a wander down the section containing the biscuits and sweet treats. She used to love digestive biscuits when she was younger. She would happily live off them now if she could, smothered in chocolate, and dipped into a hot cup of sweet tea. The thought of chocolate was beginning to make her mouth water.

She considered buying a packet of chocolate digestives to satisfy her craving, but decided against it. As soon as she opened the packet, she knew she wouldn't be able to stop at just one or two. By the time the morning arrived, she'd be faced with a pile of crumbs and an empty wrapper. Instead, she turned her attention towards the smaller bars of chocolate at the end of the aisle.

"I'm sure I can manage one of these!" she spoke to herself as she reached for a single size bar of chocolate. At least she could eat it all without feeling too guilty. She took Peter's wine and her chocolate off to the checkout.

"One of those nights, is it?" the cashier asked when she saw what Maggie had placed on the conveyor belt.

Maggie laughed a response. "I wish! The wine is for my husband. The chocolate is for me!"

"A man who drinks wine? I'm impressed!" Maggie couldn't help but notice how smiley the lady behind the till was as she beeped the items through. Her presence was comforting, Maggie felt. She wondered what it would be like to be working at this time in the evening. She wondered what it'd be like to be working at all. The cashier continued, "My partner won't drink anything but beer!"

"I'm sure my husband would drink anything if I put it in front of him, providing it had alcohol in it!" Maggie was sure she was only joking, but she was beginning to question just how much truth was in that statement.

She paid for the products and slipped the bar of chocolate in her bag. She left the bottle of wine in the carrier bag and made her way back across the car park. Peter was still listening to the radio when she climbed back into the driver's seat.

"You took your time." He switched off the radio, bored, before grabbing the carrier bag out of Maggie's hands.

Peter stumbled out of the car and slammed the door behind him. Maggie pressed the button on the car keys to lock the doors as she waited by the building; she'd already left the car and reached the door before Peter had managed to even open his side.

She held open the main door of the building for him, before following him into the flat a few seconds later. She locked the front door behind her and nipped into the bedroom to remove her shoes. By the time she reached the living room, Peter was already slumped on the sofa.

She placed her handbag in between the sofa and the door, but not before pulling out her bar of chocolate. She had been looking forward to it all the way home. "Would you like a cup of coffee, Peter?" she asked, as she stepped into the kitchen to turn the kettle on.

"Nope. The wine will do nicely!"

In truth, she didn't really feel like drinking coffee either. She just wanted Peter to drink something other than the wine in an attempt to balance out the alcohol. She hated seeing him drink. He was never very good at estimating the strength of what he was drinking, and always seemed to end up consuming too much of it. He stood up and walked into the kitchen.

"No, me neither." She sat down in the chair, and curled her legs under her. She tore open the chocolate bar's wrapper and snapped off a chunk before popping it into her mouth. She sucked on it for a moment, allowing the sugary warmth to cover her tongue as the chocolate began to melt. If only for a moment, she could escape her surroundings and ignore Peter, concentrating only on the pleasure that coated her mouth.

She drew her attention back to Peter, who returned to the sofa with a large glass of wine in his hand. "I think I might go to bed in a minute. It's been a long day."

"Whatever," Peter grizzled. He wasn't really paying attention to what Maggie was saying. He fidgeted for a moment as he sat down, unable to find a comfortable spot. "What's this?" From down the side of the sofa cushion he pulled out a small hardback book, its cover a navy blue and missing its dust-jacket. The gold lettering down the spine had started to fade.

Maggie had forgotten that she had thrown the book onto the sofa that morning when she had returned from her walk. "It's a book," she replied, bluntly.

"Give me some credit, Margaret. I'm not an idiot. I can see perfectly well that it's a book. What is it doing wedged down the side of my sofa?"

"I must have forgotten to put it away. Sorry, Peter." She pulled her knees in closer towards her chest as the air around her turned a little colder.

"Why do you even bother to read anything? Books are such a waste of time. All they will ever do is fill your head with lies." Peter opened up the book and turned to a random page. He began to read it to himself. Maggie averted her eyes from her husband, until a few moments later he continued, "What is this rubbish?! The idiot doesn't make any sense!"

"It's called *A Vindication of the Rights of Woman*. It's a book written by Mary Wollstonecraft." Maggie hesitated. "I hadn't really heard of it before, but Josie sent it in the post to me. I was just flicking through it, Peter. I wasn't really paying any attention to it." She decided not to tell him that she had actually found it to be quite an interesting read.

"Wollstonecraft? Isn't she that feminist freak from the nineteenth century or something? I remember we learned about her at school. She sounded like a right nutcase!"

"Eighteenth century." Maggie whispered timidly.

"What?"

"She was from the eighteenth century."

"You seem to know an awful lot about her considering you said you hadn't read the book." There was a hint of anger in the back of Peter's voice.

"It…I…there's a biography at the beginning." Maggie thought carefully about what she was saying, not wanting to aggravate Peter. "I was just skimming over it this morning when it was delivered." Maggie stared down at the carpet, avoiding Peter's eyes.

He slammed the book shut and threw it up into the air, catching it loudly in between his hands as it came back down. "What's Josie doing sending you books anyway?"

"She just said she thought I might enjoy reading

it. She said she found it interesting herself. I don't think I'm going to bother reading it though," she lied.

That wasn't entirely true. Josie had explained in the note she sent with the book that she thought Maggie would be able to benefit from reading it. She thought Wollstonecraft had some very inspiring views that would help empower her sister. Maggie wasn't so sure, and didn't really feel it was something she needed, but she was willing to read what the book had to say.

"I guess you don't need it lying around then." He stopped swinging the book by its spine and rose from the sofa. Carrying the book loosely between his fingers, he crossed over to the bookshelf that rested beside the chair Maggie was sitting in. He dropped it onto the bottom shelf, allowing it to land with a thud. Aside from a few old catalogues which nobody ever seemed to remember to discard, the shelves remained bare. As Peter straightened up, his eyes caught something on top of the bookcase. He looked for a moment, before asking, "What's this?"

Chewing the last piece of chocolate from her bar, Maggie turned her head to look up at Peter standing next to her. He was now holding her scrapbook in his hands, and was flicking through roughly. Maggie was silent as she searched for the best answer.

"Margaret!"

She jumped as the sound of Peter's bellow shot through her ear. Curling herself into the back of her chair, she tried to answer. "I..."

"I thought I'd told you to stop all of this nonsense?" He threw the scrapbook onto the table, and turned to face Maggie. "Didn't I?!"

"Yes, Peter, you did. I'm sorry," she sniveled a

reply, drawing her knees up to her chest, and wrapping her arms around her ankles.

Peter pressed a fist into the wooden surface of the table to support his weight, as he stood leaning over slightly to study the scrapbook. It had landed shut when he'd thrown it across the table, the front cover displaying the picture that Maggie had drawn when she was a little girl. Maggie had taken as much care as possible to save its condition. The bridge had started to fade slightly, and the corners of the page had curled a little over the years, but the woman with the wings seemed to be just as bright now as she was when Maggie first brought her to life. It was not something she had ever intended to show Peter.

She should have known better than to leave the scrapbook drying in the living room. Peter had expressed, quite clearly, that she was not to waste her time with such "pathetic child's play." He could never understand why she would even want to bother with art in the first place.

Had she not left the application forms for the art school on the living room table when Peter had arrived home from work, she may still have had the chance to send them off. To this day, she still didn't know if she would have been good enough to be offered a place those twenty years ago. It didn't really matter now though, did it?

He had accepted her love of drawing in the beginning. As long as it was only something she was going to do every now and then as a hobby, he could cope with it. When he found the forms though, something inside of him had flipped. He grabbed the pencil that she had left sitting on top of her sketchpad and snapped it straight into two pieces. There was no way that any wife of his was going to run off to spend all day drawing silly pictures. Who would keep the house tidy? Who would cook his meals? As soon as he realised Maggie wasn't just scribbling away for a hobby, he became intolerant to her passion.

He observed the woman on the front of the scrapbook. "What sort of weird creature is this meant to be?!" He looked in disgust.

"I think she's meant to be a fairy." Maggie straightened up a little in the chair. She had never talked to anybody about the picture before; it felt strange to be speaking about it now.

"What do you mean, you *think* it's a fairy? You drew the thing, didn't you?"

Maggie considered telling Peter the truth, about how she had dreamed the image. How would he react if she told him that something, somewhere in her mind, was telling her to draw her? She wasn't sure she would be able to explain it. Instead, she decided to go for a safer option and make something up. "I copied the picture from a photograph I had seen in a book when I was younger. I can't remember what it was about now though."

"Well, she doesn't look much like a fairy. She doesn't really look like anything! Her eyes are stupid. And her mouth is squint." Maggie blushed as she felt the blow of Peter's words.

As he spoke, Peter felt a sharp pang in the back of his neck. He lifted his hand and massaged it for a second. It had felt as though somebody had prodded him with a very sharp, pointed finger. Choosing not to let his imagination get the better of him, he turned his attention back to the scrapbook.

He grabbed hold of one of the corners and

flipped it over to the next page. The pastel pink card displayed a group of girls all standing in a line. Each of the five girls was wearing an evening dress. Peter spotted a younger version of his wife as she stood to the far left of the photograph. Her blonde hair was curled right down to her waist. He couldn't help but notice the way the scarlet material of her dress hugged her slim figure. All of the girls in the photo were dressed in similar shades of red, as if they had formed some kind of pact. Peter was sure he hadn't seen the picture before. "What's this from?"

Maggie unfolded her arms from around her legs and stood up from the chair. She walked over to stand next to Peter. "That was my sixth-year leaving do," she replied as she looked at the picture in the middle of the scrapbook page, a smile creeping across her face.

"Your hair doesn't look too bad there. Why don't you let your hair grow out like that now?" He turned to face her. "I don't know why you leave it in this frizzy mess." He lifted a strand of hair from her shoulder-length cut in distaste. "People must think you don't make an effort with your appearance. How do you think that makes me look?"

Maggie wanted to tell Peter than she didn't have the motivation to do anything nice with her hair. Nobody ever made her feel pretty, and so she didn't really feel like there was any need to spend hours doing her hair or make-up. She knew she shouldn't say that to him though. "I don't really have the time to style longer hair every morning," she said instead.

"What do you mean, you don't have the time? You spend all day in the house. Of course you do!"

She couldn't believe what she was hearing. Was

he really accusing her of wasting the time away? Did he really think she spent all day alone by choice? She couldn't keep her voice inside of her as the frustration and anger boiled. "That's only because you won't let me work!" she shouted, before she realised what she was doing. Maggie threw her hand in front of her mouth. It was too late. She'd already said it.

"Excuse me? I won't let you work?! No, Margaret!" His words were sharp as they hit Maggie in the face. Peter pushed the wooden chair into the table, causing it to rattle with the impact. "You are very, very mistaken, Margaret. You are my wife!" He spat at her as he bellowed right into her face. "When you married me, you made your decision! It is not that I won't let you work, you stupid woman!" He jabbed at Maggie's chest with an outstretched index finger. She stumbled back slightly, not fully prepared for the outburst. "It's your duty to serve me, and you know that perfectly well. Don't you?"

Maggie was silent, unable to find any words to respond. She stared into the corner of the room where the television was positioned. Peter stepped in front of her as if to block her view. He held her chin in between his fingers and pulled her face forwards him so that she was forced to look straight at him. Her eyes were filled with tears.

She could smell the strong stench of wine on his breath as he exhaled close to her face. "Margaret, I said you know it's your duty to serve me, don't you?!"

She tried to speak, but her mouth had become dry. "I…" she whispered.

"Answer me!" Peter shouted in her face. Maggie watched in fear as his eyes flared with rage. She continued to watch as he lifted his hand in the air. She took everything in as if it was happening in slow motion. She could see what was unfolding, but she was frozen to the spot. She was too frightened; there was nothing she could do to stop it. She watched as Peter swung his heavy hand down through the air towards her cheek. He struck it hard across her face. The collision shook right through her entire body. Maggie let out a scream as it knocked her to the floor, the pain of the impact with the solid ground ringing in her ears as she lay there, sobbing, unable to move.

Chapter Three

The cold air that once took hold of the room begins to heat up around me. The inside of my walls grow into a fiery pit. I can feel my skin burning. It is crawling, searching of cool relief. But the air does not cooperate.

A pain soars across my face. It smothers my mind in a blanket of anxiety. I wish this was a new experience. I wish I was not familiar with the prickly heat that has emerged on the surface of my cheeks. I know this feeling all too well.

There is nothing that I can do except wait. Time will pass. It always does. In the back of my mind, the sound of the clock ceases to escape from me. I can hear it, constantly ticking. Each strike counts away the seconds of my existence.

Tick.

Tick.

Tick.

It is not counting down how long I have left. It does not indicate when I will be allowed freedom from the aches of my own reality. Instead, each second exists to remind me of how long I have been stuck, trapped within my own four walls.

Bruises form against my burning skin. I can feel the ground beginning to cut deeper into me as I struggle to move. The fragile shards of broken stone continue to attack the backs of my legs. I try to stand up; I need to ease the pain, but a lack of energy strikes me back down. I have nothing else to give. It knocks me onto my side. I am instantly sent into agony as I collide with the concrete. I can feel the fresh mark on my skin knitting together as I press my hand against the bottom of my rib cage. It is just a bruise. It is not cracked. Nothing is broken. Not yet. Not this time.

I tell myself that I am fine. I struggle through the pain to bend my knees as I curl upright. I manage to return myself to sitting, so that I'm in a ball with my back arched against the wall. If I do not try to move – if I do not take any risks – I am sure I'll be okay.

I long to scream, to shout out, but nobody will hear me. There is nobody around. Nobody who can pick me up and carry me. I haven't the strength to cry out. I can only weep silently as I cling on to my last ounce of hope that somebody, somewhere, will find me and take me away to safety.

I've stopped wondering why. I know better now than to ask questions. I have learned that the hard way. It is easier to just sit here, as I rock back and forth, absorbed in my own silence. Silence is something that cannot hurt me. I am allowed to rest in the quiet space of my own company.

But I loathe the silence. It must be questioned why it is so quiet. When there is nothing to hear, the air is filled with a chill of uncertainty. It indicates that a storm is waiting to happen. I am alone and abandoned before I am forced to stand and fight.

Except I do not have the strength to fight. I can barely hold myself up as I rest on the ground. There is nothing I can do about it. I have to accept that this is the way it is meant to be. I know I must go on. I know I must try and fight it. But in my weakness I know that it is here that I must remain. It is here that I must live. It is here that I must die.

The thought of leaving this place terrifies me. I hate being here, but I've grown used to it. There is an order to my loneliness. The routine is comforting; I know what to expect when I am here. When I am locked in here, I don't have to worry about what lies outside. Except that I do worry. I always will.

He escapes free outside, but he cannot hurt me here. He thinks he can. He thinks he can creep his way inside and break up my loneliness, my existence. But he can't. He has bruised me on the outside. He has crushed me so many times before. I may not be able to escape these walls, but at least I know that I am safe from his grasp while I am in here.

I can often hear him, shouting and screaming somewhere in the distance from the outside. He sometimes bangs his fists against the brickwork to try and get to me, but he never succeeds. It angers him. It frustrates him. His voice rises as he struggles to infiltrate his way inside.

Within my walls, the pain he inflicts upon me is only superficial. I know that it can't last. He will not last.

But how I long to burst through the barriers. I ache to run free from this dark and desolate space. But I must stay. I have soaked the ground in my tears. I have pasted the soil into a salty mud. I have swept the dust with the shards of my soul that he has broken. I breathe, and that is all. But at least I breathe.

As I lift my head, I am sure I can see something. Out of the corner of my eye, I notice that there is something beside me. I can sense it. I don't know what it is. I can't seem to look at it directly. Something is stopping me from turning my head. Instead, I close my eyes tightly shut.

Nothing has ever been able to get inside my walls before. I know it is not him; I would be able to hear him. I would hear his heavy breathing as he beats down on me. I want to open my eyes and look at it. I want to see its face. Does it have a face? I can sense it moving closer. It is right behind me now. It stands over my shoulder.

I'm not scared. I know it's nothing to fear. And yet, I don't know why I can't look at it. What if it's here to take me away? I don't want to leave. I am not ready. It can't take me away. What does it want with me? I still don't understand how it managed to get in. There is no entrance. There is no exit. Just four walls.

My four walls.

I find myself beginning to rock back and forth softly as I hug my knees. No, I mustn't open my eyes. I can't. I am not ready.

Not ready for what? I am overcome with a strange sensation. There is no fear within me. For the first time in more years than I can remember I find myself calm. I do not feel worried. I am not afraid of this thing that has joined me. I am not concerned about what has entered my space. But my eyes remain closed.

They begin to water. No, they are not watering. I am crying. I begin to weep. The tears fall as if all of my emotions have at once rushed to my surface. I sob silently to myself for reasons I cannot explain.

I long to open my eyes. I take a deep breath and pull myself together. I manage to stop sobbing as I try to control my surge of emotions.

In the distance, I can hear something. Listen. There's a sound. It's a sort of soft twinkling noise. It's so gentle, so pretty. What is it? It's so faint. With my eyes closed, I am able to concentrate on the sound. I am sure that, in the distance, I can hear the soft drone of an organ.

A violin. It is such a sweet sound. It's relaxing, soothing. It doesn't screech or scratch at me at all.

Silence.

The music has stopped. My walls have restored the quiet that they usually possess. I find myself missing, instantly, the comforting presence of the sound. The instruments were delicate, touching. I've no clue where it came from, but I hope it returns soon.

For a moment I seemed to have forgotten about the thing that had managed to enter through my walls. I wonder if it's still here. Perhaps it left with the music. I can only assume that the two arrived together.

No, I can still feel it. I can almost sense it touching me, but it does not quite do so. I must not look yet.

My attention is drawn back to my surroundings as the silence of the atmosphere is replaced with invasive noise. I open my eyes. Any sense of the unknown presence has vanished, and I am alone in here once more. Outside my walls, I can hear him. The glass clinks against the bottle. I do not want to hear this. Oh how I long for the sweet mysterious music to return. Please, let me listen to the gentle sounds again. Anything to block out the chaos of the world outside.

He is pouring it. He is drinking it. It is my own fault. Nobody else is to blame. I am to blame. Idiot. He is immune from its poison; it is me who becomes drenched instead, as it soaks through my pours and into my heart. It makes its way into my mind. It attacks my soul.

I start to lose all sense of the safety of my walls. I can taste the smoke as I breathe in. I am forced to inhale it deep into my lungs as it infiltrates into the space around me. The threatening taste smothers me as I search for fresh air. I feel suffocated. I want out. I continue to rock back and forth. Forward. And back. Forward. And back. There is no safety. There is no escape. I am trapped and I don't know where I am.

Chapter Four

He crossed his left leg over the other, and started to tap his foot profusely against the front of the sofa. His boots were starting to wear away at the soles, but he refused to buy a new pair, despite Maggie's attempts to encourage him to do so. Peter had decided that as long as his boots were solid where they were visible, then they were adequate enough. They were still in one piece, so why should he spend money on something he felt he neither needed nor wanted?

He pulled the ashtray slightly closer to him from where he had let it rest on the arm of the sofa. Turning it round, he made the lip of the tray face him so that it was more conveniently accessed. Between his right fingers he held a second cigarette, this one freshly lit. He placed it in between his lips, moistening the tip slightly and drawing in his breath sharply. Slowly he exhaled, allowing the smoke to circulate around him. It drifted out and began to make its way around the room. "You know," he began, "I'm sure these used to taste different." He flicked ash into the glass tray beside him. "I swear they used to taste more... I don't know, non-artificial. Now I can barely taste anything other than the cardboard from the packet. And I don't know why they bother to put all these silly warning labels on them." He glared down at the grey packed that sat in his lap. The top half was opened to reveal the remaining four cigarettes. "I mean, who is it going to make any difference to? They're just wasting their time. Whoever *they* are. What sort of job is that? 'Oh, what did you do at work today, Steve?' 'You'll never guess! I put another warning label on the front of a packet of fags. I've never had so much fun!'?'" Peter mocked snidely. Another flick of ash went into the tray.

Reaching down, he picked up the glass that he had left by his feet. He brought the glass to his lips to take a sip of the liquid. The wine trickled down his throat, attempting to coat it in the comforting sensation he so frequently experienced. "There's nothing finer than a fine glass of wine," he'd often joke, laughing before adding, "and this is not a fine glass of wine!"

Today, Peter didn't think that it was a particularly fine glass of wine. It was making him feel quite bitter, despite the fact that he seemed to be drowning himself in it. "Why did you buy this stuff, Margaret? It's absolutely disgusting." He took another drink from the glass. He swirled around the rest of the drink that lay in the bottom of it, watching it as it splashed up and down the sides. "I bet it was cheap. You never buy the good stuff. What have I always said? When it comes to my wine, you can't just buy the rubbish that's on offer. There's a reason that they're trying to get rid of it by the bucket-load. No, Margaret, from now on, you better make sure that you damn well buy the decent stuff." He drained the glass, and crushed the last of his cigarette into the ashtray.

He pressed his arm into the side of the sofa to lift himself up. He proceeded to cross over towards the table, where he carelessly placed the glass down onto the wooden surface. Maggie's scrapbook still lay across the table where Peter had discarded it earlier. "I'm bored. Let's see what else is in this, shall we?"

Maggie remained in her own silence as she sat in the chair next to the bookshelf, keeping her knees tucked under her chin as she hugged herself. She continued to stare into space, her body as motionless as her mind seemed to be, as Peter hastily pulled the scrapbook towards him. She couldn't bring herself to look at him. She tried to fight the taste of cigarette that had intruded its way into her mouth, but it was pointless. The air was thick with Peter's foul second-hand smoke.

Peter snorted as he looked down at her scrapbook. Sometimes he just couldn't believe Maggie at all. He couldn't establish why anybody would waste their time working on such dire scrap. "I bet all of this art tat wasn't cheap either, was it? Remind me, please, Margaret. At what point did I give you permission to waste away my money – that's money that I work exceptionally hard for day in day out – on all of this junk?" He ran a dirty, nicotine-stained finger over the grooves of the little flower that had been embossed into a sheet of cream card. "Margaret, you will answer me!"

Knowing better than to ignore the aggressive vibrations in Peter's voice, Maggie slowly lifted her head and forced her eyes to meet his, if only just for a second. Peter was holding up the scrapbook loosely in one hand to indicate to Maggie which particular waste of time and money he was referring to just now. Maggie recognised it instantly.

Twenty-one years ago she sat herself down with all of her craft tools surrounding her to work on that collage. Her sister had bought her the most wonderful pack of delicate ivory and cream sheets of card. Each one was embossed with either roses or lilies. She thought they were the some of the most gorgeous materials she had ever seen; she was almost too scared to touch them. She couldn't wait to pour her memories and creativity into them.

She stared now at the object that sat in the middle of the collage. She could feel Peter's eyes burrowing into her mind, demanding that she provide him with an answer to his sour question. But she knew that nothing she said would be good enough. No answer she could ever give would satisfy him. As she gazed at the picture's centerpiece, she managed to whisper out a response softly for Peter. "Do you remember the ribbon?"

He stared at her, a look of confused spread across his face. "The ribbon?! What on earth are you blabbering on about, Margaret?!"

She knew before the words had even left her mouth that she had said the wrong thing. She had to continue though. Swallowing away the feelings of timidity, she explained. "The ribbon around the cake. Do you remember it?" She nodded towards the image of a three-tier wedding cake that she had positioned in the center of the scrapbook page. She'd taken a photo of the cake on the day with the idea in mind that she would use it especially for a feature in her scrapbook to help log the occasion that was set to be the happiest day of her life. The following week, once she had the few photographs that she'd taken developed, she spent an entire afternoon putting everything together while Peter was at work. She took great care in trimming around the shape of the cake, making sure she didn't slice off any of the delicate curves of the icing that were displayed proudly on top of a silver platter. She glued the cut out photo into the middle of the cream card; she had decided to use the one with the roses as they matched with the delicate little pink icing flowers that decorated the top of the middle layer of the wedding cake.

She'd remembered to save the silver ribbon from around the large bottom tier to use for her artwork, fashioning it into a border for the base layer of the cake in the photo. As Peter swung the scrapbook about in front of her, Maggie could still make out a hint of the shimmer in its sparkly edges as the light hit it.

Peter was taken aback by his wife's seemingly stupid question. "No, of course I don't remember a piece of ugly ribbon!" he grunted at her. He placed the scrapbook back down on the table, a little more gently this time than the force with which he had previously thrust it into the air. He was lying about the ribbon, and Maggie knew it.

It had happened after the wedding reception,

after the champagne toasts and the three-course meal. Everybody had gone home by this point. Maggie and Peter were alone together; they were the only two left on the dance floor, the DJ having vacated ten minutes earlier. The room now stood in silence.

They'd agreed to meet Josie with her partner for a few drinks afterwards to end the evening. Peter couldn't remember her partner's name, even on the day; she had had so many over the years that he struggled to keep up. He dreaded to think how many names had been added to the list since she had moved to London.

Josie had insisted that she had to toast her sister and new brother-in-law for a second time a little more intimately in their favourite local pub on the high street. Before they all headed off, though, Maggie and Peter had decided to spend a few moments together on their own. Maggie was still in her wedding dress, and didn't have any plans to change out of it before they went to the pub. Peter swore that he had never seen a vision more attractive before. Maggie – no, he made sure he corrected himself - his *wife* was as beautiful as a swan. She was even more beautiful, in fact. She was perfect.

Maggie had chosen a simple white satin dress for her wedding day. It graced the floor gently as she walked, sweeping ever so slightly behind her feet, swaying elegantly around her ankles as she moved. She knew Peter wouldn't want her to wear anything too revealing, and especially not on the most important day of their lives together where everybody would be looking at her, so she had decided that the lace sleeves and matching neckline would be a nice touch to the dress. If she was being completely honest with herself, it wouldn't have been her first choice, but it was all that she could really afford with the budget that Peter had allowed her. She'd managed to find a pair of delicate cream suede shoes in the local charity shop that looked as though they had been worn just one time; she fell in love with their tiny little heels almost immediately, so she didn't feel too bad about having to wear second hand shoes for her wedding. And at the end of the day, Peter was proud to be seen with her, which was the most important factor for Maggie. Yes, he was sure that his bride looked more wonderful and graceful than he could have ever imagined. He couldn't have felt any luckier.

His luck started to fade, however, once he decided to try on the ribbon. "I bet I can do it, Margaret!" he assured her. "Just you watch!" He slipped the ribbon over his head, the ends still connected together. He let it sit loosely around his neck for a second as he took his bride's hand and twirled her around in a circle. "See, it fits!"

"It's only over your head, silly!" she giggled. She thought he looked ever so funny with the ribbon from the cake hanging down. "That wasn't what I had dared you to do, was it?"

"Okay, have it your way, Mrs Gordon!" He emphasised her name with pride. "Are you ready to watch the magic happen?" Peter stood for a moment, flexing his arms as if to show off his muscles through his suit. The champagne had sent him into a playful mood, which caused him to chuckle to himself every few moments. "Well? Are you ready?"

"I'm ready!"

"One... two... three!" Peter flung his right arm

through the ribbon, wearing it for a moment like a very tight sash. He struggled with his left arm as he attempted to weave it through the ribbon.

Maggie watched in amusement, only ever so slightly concerned. "Peter, I don't think..."

"Hang on, I've nearly got it!" He continued to battle with the cake ribbon for a few moments. Maggie had to force herself to not burst out laughing. "There, I've done it!"

Finally, Peter had managed to manoeuvre the ribbon down his arm, rather than trying to pull his arm through it. He was just able to slip his hand out so that the ribbon was now sat around his waist. Maggie couldn't keep the laughter in any longer.

"Margaret Gordon, do you find your husband's amazing ribbon belt amusing?" Peter joked as he pulled Maggie close to him. He held her for a moment as they stood in the center of the room, alone and swaying in the mutuality of their happiness.

Of course, Peter hadn't thought too far ahead with this venture. He soon realised that the ribbon was now stuck around his waist. Maggie refused to let him rip it – it had been fixed together neatly with the edges lining up perfectly, and tugging at it would only tear it up. There didn't seem to be a pair of scissors anywhere nearby to make a neat cut down the side of it either, so Maggie had made him wear the ribbon for the rest of the evening. He'd agreed to do so, but only on the condition that she stayed in her wedding dress.

"Fine by me!" Maggie had replied, waltzing around the empty hall. She loved the sound her shoes made as they clacked against the polished wooden surface. Each step echoed loudly around the room as she danced. And so they both turned up to the pub that evening to meet Josie, Maggie still in her wedding dress and Peter in his ribbon, both of them the happiest that they had ever been.

Peter turned his attention to the invitation that was mounted onto the scrapbook card. It was positioned just to the left above of the photograph of the cake. Maggie had tucked a corner of the spare invitation under the top layer, and had fastened it shut with a little sticker of a red love-heart. Peter noticed that Maggie had written the initials *MG* onto the center of the heart in swirly gold lettering.

He wondered if it had been the first time that she had written her initials with his surname. He glanced over to where she sat in the corner of the room. She'd turned her attention back to the floor now; when Peter had not been able to answer her truthfully about the ribbon, she had retreated back into herself where she silently began to recall her wedding day in her mind. She thought of the smiling faces of the guests that shone at her as she walked nervously down the aisle; the look of pride on Peter's face as he turned to look at her when she approached him; the hideously puffy lilac bridesmaids' dresses she made Josie and Lucy wear which still made her laugh; the way she could see her cousin Billy, twelve years her junior, sitting picking his nose out of the corner of her eye throughout the entire reception. It was a day she treasured so dearly in her heart; it allowed her to experience emotions she knew she would never be able to recreate.

How many of these invitations had been sent out? Peter wondered. He was sure it had been too many, however many it was. He had never really wanted a big wedding, but when Maggie started to list all of the family members she simply couldn't miss off the guest list, and then included all of the 'plus one' guests that she was too polite to leave out, Peter knew that he was going to have to be prepared to pay out for a pretty big wedding. He didn't see why they couldn't just get married in a registry office and be done with it. In the end, though, he had enjoyed the day, or at least towards the end of it once he was finally allowed a drink. But he was still annoyed at the fact that it could have easily cost him half as much if he had just put his foot down. He told himself the next morning, when the hangover from the lavish celebrations had kicked in and he discovered drowning an entire carton of orange juice was the only way to ease the pain, that he would just have to be more strict with Maggie in the future.

Peter spotted in the corner of the page a small drawing of two rings. Unlike most of the other images on the collage, which had been cut out of photographs or bridal magazines, or had been leftover souvenirs from the wedding, Maggie had formed these little rings by hand. He looked down at his own ring. He'd barely taken it off over the years; it had almost become a part of him, at one with his left hand. He twisted the band a few times round his finger. What would it feel like if he were to take it off? He imagined it would leave him feeling quite naked, as if a large part of him had been removed. Wearing the ring gave him power. It gave him control.

For the first time, Peter noticed how old and worn his ring had started to appear. The two rings in Maggie's drawing remained shining in the excitement and innocence of their newness. It was almost as if time had not been given a chance to attack the beauty of the rings, allowing them to remain pure and free from the decomposition of life. How long had it been since he'd asked her to marry him? He was barely able to remember how he'd even proposed to her. He could recall that it had been raining that day. Maggie had spent most of the evening gazing out of the window, rambling on about how she loved the way the droplets of rain rested against the leaves as they landed on the trees and on the plants. It was something like that, anyway, he thought to himself. She'd cooked them both a meal, some pasta dish with Bolognese sauce. Or did it have a tuna base? The evening was hazy in his mind. He was sure there was wine though. Yes, he was positive that there had been wine then too.

He had to be honest with himself and admit that he hadn't really given a lot of thought to the proposal, or even to the idea of marriage itself. He hadn't been dating Maggie for very long, fewer than twelve months if he remembered correctly. Peter had certainly found her to be very pretty, there was no denying that. Her bright blonde hair had been newly cut short, much shorter than it was now, and she had it styled in lots of little layers at the back. He loved the playful youthfulness about her. In fact, the bounciness of her energy was one of the first things that had attracted him to her. He'd been in the library in town, searching for books that would tell him all he wanted to know about setting up his own business from scratch, when he became distracted by the vision sifting through a shelf of books in the corner of the room. Maggie had been wearing a pair of baggy jeans that sat gently around her waist, and her oversized jumper hung carefree off one shoulder.

Peter found himself instantly attracted to her.

When Peter had proposed to Maggie, she was no longer wearing jeans. She sat that evening in a figure-hugging black dress decorated with little diamante studs across its thin straps. She still possessed the fun young vibe that Peter had originally been drawn to, but she somehow now looked more mature. She appeared more grown up. Peter couldn't help but notice this as he admired how finely her ladylike curves shaped the silk fabric of her outfit. As he chewed on a mouthful of food, he stared in wonder at the sight displayed in front of him. He'd decided in that moment that she was the woman he was going to transform into his wife.

Having only recently left school, Maggie hadn't exactly planned on finding herself walking down the aisle at any time soon, but she had agreed to marry Peter almost the second that the question had left his lips. She felt she could trust him, and had decided that spending the rest of her life with him would consist of all things wonderful and nothing less. She would still go to art school as she had planned, of course, and then perhaps she might consider training to become an art teacher. Peter could still go about setting up his business, just as soon as he'd decided what exactly he wanted that business to focus on; Maggie ignored the fact that Peter didn't really know anything about running a business. It didn't matter though, as she knew they'd have the most perfect life together. It didn't occur to Maggie at the time that plans don't always work out the way they were intended to.

Peter looked over at Maggie now as she sat in the chair, still clutching at herself. Her arms were wrapped protectively around her ankles. Her eyes remained focused on the floor. There seemed to be a distinctive lack of life in them that Peter failed to notice. Maggie's own rings had never left her left hand. Her engagement ring and wedding band alike seemed to look a lot brighter to Peter than his own did.

Abandoning the scrapbook for a moment, he crossed over to the other side of the room to where the wine bottle sat so that he could fill his glass again. He stood still for a moment, glass in hand, thinking about nothing in particular. He gulped down a mouthful of the liquid, and then proceeded immediately to drain the glass before filling it up straight away again. As if out of nowhere, he turned to look at Maggie. "Why did you change?"

Maggie heard what Peter had said. Her mind started to work overtime as she tried to search for an answer, but nothing seemed to come to her. She didn't really understand the question she was being asked. She continued to look down at the floor, though her eyes were flickering back and forth in a desperate attempt to find something, anything, to say in response. She hoped Peter was asking her rhetorically, but she doubted it.

"Look at you here." He was leaning against the table again as he jabbed a finger at the photo that took pride of place in the center of the next page in Maggie's scrapbook. Peter had turned the page over to reveal their wedding photo. Maggie had kept this page simple, mounting the photograph of the happy couple onto a piece of red cardboard which she'd cut with crinkly scissors into the shape of a love-heart. She had glued it onto a sheet of sparkly silver card before adding the page to the rest in the scrapbook. She had decided that it didn't need any frills. The two smiling faces that shone out of the photograph were enough to light up the entire page. Maggie had intended to design the simple collage to be a memory of the start of their beautiful lives together, but it rather now remained a symbol of what could have been. It displayed a hope that she found she was no longer able to cherish.

"This is the woman I married." Maggie winced when she heard the slur in the end of Peter's sentence. She tried to work out how much he'd had to drink, but couldn't concentrate on any numbers to try and calculate it properly. "See this woman here, Margaret?" Peter pointed to the photo, not paying attention to whether or not Maggie had turned to look at him. "She was absolutely beautiful. She was so petite, so full of life. Her hair bounced when she walked; she'd move around with a little skip in her step, almost as if somebody had fastened tiny springs to the bottom of her shoes. She would always have the biggest smile across her face. She was always smiling, always laughing. And you should have seen her eyes, Margaret. They were like two large saucers, each one bursting with curiosity, each glistening bright with life. I can't remember what colour they were now. I don't think they had a particular colour now that I think about it; she was always as colourful as a rainbow. I didn't need to search for the pot of gold at the end of the rainbow, because I already had it. All the wealth in the world, she brought to me. All the wealth in the world. What happened, Margaret?"

He was standing in front of her now. He'd left the scrapbook on the table, the memory of their wedding day abandoned and staring up at the ceiling. He had refused to leave his glass behind, however. He drained it once more, before slammed it down onto the table behind him.

"Margaret!"

Maggie jumped, causing her legs to slide out of the grasp of her arms. She folded forward slightly against her own will, closer towards Peter. In the moment, he grabbed hold of the tops of her arms and dragged her upright onto her feet. His hands clenched tight around her arms as she shook her slightly. "Why did you change, Margaret?! I used to love you!"

He surprised himself when he forced her against the wall, causing the lower part of her back to bend against the solid radiator that was situated next to the chair she had been sitting in. The tears rolled down her cheeks as Peter's words stung through her, but still she remained silent. She was too scared to make a sound, unsure of how Peter would respond. She was screaming inside, though. She was desperate for him to let go of her, to loosen his grip so that the tops of her arms would stop throbbing. She could smell the alcohol on his breath as he moved in closer to her face. It made her want to throw up, but she clenched her stomach inside of her, holding everything together, bundling it alongside the cries she longed to release.

"You used to be so pretty, Margaret. I used to be proud to call you my wife. But look at you now. You're a disgusting mess!" He released his grip and stepped back slightly, still holding on to stop his wife from going anywhere. Maggie stood shaking, too frightened to attempt to move. She continued to lean with her back against the wall as Peter studied her.

"You really do embarrass me, Margaret." He lifted up a strand of her hair before letting it fall down again. "What kind of colour do you call this? It looks like you haven't washed it in weeks! And what's all that filthy dark stuff growing from your roots?! How do you expect me to introduce you to people and tell them that you're my wife when you don't even know how to present yourself properly? You're a disgrace, Margaret. Remember how your hair used to be? It used to be soft and shiny. Why have you let it grow into straw, Margaret? Why?"

Maggie couldn't hold it together any longer, as she lost control of the small hold she had managed to keep over her emotions as she burst into tears. Her sobs grew louder as she gave up fighting to keep it inside of her, drained of all energy.

Her sudden outburst sent Peter into a rage. He almost pounced onto her as he lunged his right hand forward and grabbed hold of her jaw. He held her there, pressing his weight against her so that she was pinned against the wall. The sudden fright caused by Peter's actions stunned her into silence.

She could feel his entire body shaking. He wasn't sure what he was doing, or why he was doing it, but something refused to let him back down. His eyes pierced into hers as they stood there in silence. He noticed the fear behind her own eyes as his grip started to tighten against her neck.

It was only when an unexpected single tear rolled down Peter's cheek that he found the strength within himself to loosen his grip. He stepped away from Maggie as he wiped his face. Exhausted, she slumped to the floor. She rubbed at the red marks that had emerged around her neck. She watched, still overcome with terror, as Peter reached for another glass of wine. She realised now that she was unsure of what her husband was capable of. She had always been quite scared of him, and considered herself used to his outbursts, but for the first time she found herself fearing for her life.

She let her own tears fall down, smothering her guilt as she searched for an answer.

Chapter Five

The darkness that rests behind my eyes has increased. Just open your eyes, Maggie, I promise you'll be safe. It has been so many years now. So many long, tiresome years. I was too young. I've been able to see that for a long time now, but I struggle to change the past. I thought my beautiful, shining ring was eternal, never to be broken. It still looks full, complete. But looks are often deceitful. It is tainted with the invisible scars of my own heartache. Oh, how I long to snap it in two. I yearn to break the chain, but I do not have the strength to do so. It sharply attacks the wishes of my heart, digging in deeper and deeper with each turn. No longer does it understand me. It cannot hear me now; it does not acknowledge my cries, but still it refuses to leave me alone.

I sense that I'm no longer alone again. A faint

trickle of light has made its way through the blackness. I've found the strength to open my eyes again, as something outside of me encourages me to do so. Just behind my left shoulder, I can detect the figure once more. I know I need to turn round and look at it this time. Yes, I'm certain I must turn around.

To my surprise, I find that I am suddenly no longer able to feel the full force of the broken particles of rock that have always sat beneath me. It's almost as if they are no longer present. I place my hand below as I feel for the jagged shapes. They prick me slightly, reassuring me that they are still there. Somehow, they don't hurt as much now though; it's as though somebody has sanded them down when I wasn't looking, easing the pain a little to help protect me.

The small thread of light that still trickles down from behind me has started to spread. It's almost a shining silver now, and has begun to curve itself around me softly. I can feel that it's a warmth as much as it is a brightness. There is a special tingling quality to it that I cannot explain. For some reason I feel safe in its strength, safer than I've ever felt throughout my entire existence. I must turn round and see where it's coming from. I must face the figure that stands beside me. I know I must turn myself around so that I can face it and...

I am looking right at her.

I have never seen a vision more beautiful before, in all of my life. She is absolutely sensational. I look at her now; it is not possible for me to turn my attention away from her. I have become transfixed as I stare up at her. I sit cross-legged as I gaze; the room is now filled with a great warmth that masks the usual chill of the draft that so often circulates around me. I don't know how, but I'm certain that she is the provider of this warmth, this comfort that has come to accompany me. She is the reason I'm overcome with a peculiar sense of protection. She is...

She is an angel!

I blink several times, struggling to believe what I am seeing. There is an *angel* standing in front of me, looking down on me. Can this really be true? Am I really in the presence of an angel? I know that these questions come naturally to me, and yet, for some reason, I find that I don't need to question her. In my heart I know that she has been sent from the heavens. It is a truth I know, and yet one I cannot explain.

As I look up at her with admiration I notice that she appears to look just like a woman. She resembles a human just like I am, but there is something spectacular about her presence that confirms for me that she is so much greater than that. I find myself glancing down at her feet. I am amazed by what I see. She appears to be hovering in the air. As she floats, her feet remain a few inches safely above the dirty ground. Resting on the floor beneath her is a small pool of soft light. It is coloured somewhere between a gentle glowing yellow, and a bright shining silver. I've never seen a shade quite like it. This same light appears to be illuminating all the way around her. It's identical to the same light that made its way towards me when she was standing behind me. The tips of my own bare toes are now tickled slightly by the delicate glow. They tingle as the light strokes at my skin.

As I turn my attention back towards her face, I notice that the angel is quite a bit taller than I am. Her height does not intimidate me though. Instead, I feel very safe with her standing by me, as if she is offering me some great protection that I cannot describe. I follow the shape of her dress as it glides all the way down her frame until it reaches her petite ankles. Although there is no wind in here, and only ever a faint draft, I'm sure that I can see her dress flowing back and forth as she stands perfectly still, as if she carries her own cooling breeze with her wherever she goes.

I always imagined that the dresses worn by angels were pure white. This is what we were always taught in school, at least, so I never really considered questioning it. This angel's dress, however, is a very delicate powdered baby blue. It almost appears to be glowing slightly, illuminated. Around the neckline of the dress I notice a gold decoration, which appears to be an inch or so thick. Upon it rests a pattern of tiny royal blue stones, each one spread an even distance from the rest, with little pearls positioned in between them. They twinkle faintly whenever she moves. I can't help but stare as I take in their beauty with admiration; I absorb their charm for as long as I can, unable to avert my eyes.

If you had asked me if I thought one's hair could be purely golden, I would have said it wasn't possible. Only now do I find that I have been very wrong, for the angel who stands in front of me has the most wonderful hair I have ever seen. It is unmistakably rich in its dazzling tones. Wavy and glossy, it cascades down her shoulders, flowing rhythmically in time with the motions of her dress. It's almost as if every part of her is connected in motion with the rest. Her hair shapes around her face so that the gentle curves of her cheeks are framed by the softness of her hair, highlighting the elegance of her dainty features.

It suddenly occurs to me that I have only just noticed the large wings that are flowing from out of her back. I'm certain that they've been here all of this time; I'm sure I could see them out of the corner of my eye. Yet it is only now that I have been drawn to look at them. It's almost as if I was temporarily not allowed to acknowledge this part of her while I grew accustomed to her being here, standing right in front of me.

Never before have I seen a set of wings, not in any artwork or depiction, so magnificent. They look as if they're growing right out of the angel's shoulders. As I think this, though, the angel turns herself ever so slightly onto an angle, as if on cue with my misconception, so that I can see that this is, in fact, not the case. The wings actually look as though they are attached to the back of her dress, sewn on to the material, but somehow I become aware that they are actually a part of her body. They curve at the top, symmetrical in shape and size, as they cascade down either side of her. They both flick into a gentle curve at the bottom, in level with her knees.

For whatever reason, I had always imagined the wings of angels to be relatively small, but these are wonderfully grand. As I am allowed the time to study them more closely, I can see that they are made up of lots of dainty little feathers. Each one is equal in size to the other, and they cannot be any greater than five or six inches in length. Upon first inspection, the angel's wings appear to be a pure white, but as I lean slightly closer towards them, I can see that the feathers are remarkably almost translucent. The edges of the wings are decorated with an illuminated sparkle of silver. They seem so delicate, but at the same time I sense that they are more powerful than I ever could imagine.

I suddenly become overwhelmed with a desire to reach out and touch them, but I cannot seem to bring myself to do so. Something tells me that this is something I'm not allowed to do; there's a force holding my actions back. It doesn't hurt, but I know my own hands must not touch the wings of the angel.

I find myself looking directly into her eyes. They are so warm and welcoming, full of more love than any human could ever possibly possess. There doesn't appear to be any colour to them, yet they also seem to display every colour in the world. They are magical. Mesmerising. There is a great tranquility to them. I allow them to soothe me as the angel looks back at me, losing myself for a moment in their peacefulness. It almost feels as though I am staring into a pond; beneath the surface I know that it's so alive and busy, but on top of the surface it is quiet and still. They flood me with an overwhelming sense of calm. It's a sensation like no other that I have ever experienced.

The angel is smiling down at me. Her lips are dainty, her smile warm and friendly. I've nothing to fear when she is in front of me. I find myself suddenly beginning to question why she is here, aware again of my surroundings. I wonder why an angel would come down from the heavens to visit me. For as long as I can remember I've sat here among the broken rocks, the darkness and the dirt that engulfs the room digging away from the outside in. But this angel has come along now, and with her she has brought new light onto my hopes.

I sit here in complete disbelief. I'm too shocked to say anything. I want to talk to her, to ask her a thousand questions, but I cannot find any words. What's the etiquette for addressing an angel? Should I be on my hands and knees at her feet? I begin to worry, unsure of how I should be presenting myself.

But this vision is so beautiful, so spectacular, that I can't seem to sustain my worry. The splendor before me is so wonderful that I would ordinarily question it, but the beauty of this angelic being is extraordinary; it has taken over all of my emotions. She lifts me up from the inside.

Before I am even given the chance to begin to doubt my own eyesight, the angel speaks to me.

Her voice is soft. I become transfixed with each word that floats out of her. The words are laced with such sweet harmony, but they project such great eloquence too. She tells me her name is Angel Ariana. She almost whispers it to me, the delicacy of her name enveloping me in her love.

She explains to me that her beautiful name is of Greek origin. She tells me that it means *very holy one*. This description makes me smile; I don't think I could ever dispute such a statement as I sit here taking in the magnificent light that surrounds her.

Angel Ariana explains that she is my guardian angel. I always wondered if guardian angels existed but was never sure; I had read one or two things about them but didn't really understand how they worked. My guardian angel senses that this news brings some confusion in me. She explains to me that she has always been in the background of my life, watching me as I have progressed through my journey. She lets me know that, even before I was born, she was around, waiting for me to grow into the world. She has always been with me, by my side, when I have needed her. It is her duty. But now she has been asked to step forward and make herself known to me. She is here to help me.

She allows me to take a moment for her message to sink in. To consider that I have walked through life with Angel Ariana by my side starts to baffle me. I know I shouldn't doubt the information, but I can't work it out inside my head how this is possible. Surely I would have sensed her, or even seen her at some point.

She tells me that I am to trust her, and that I have nothing to fear.

Angel Ariana voices my name now. *Maggie Fallon*. She speaks softly, her words soothing around me. She explains that I must listen to her; she is here to guide me. She will show me the way.

I watch as Angel Ariana lifts her right arm forward into the air. The long sleeve of her dress floats elegantly as she moves. She looks at me with warmth in her eyes as I sit in front of her with my legs crossed, too much in awe to move or speak. My hands are pressed against the floor behind me. I can no longer feel the intrusion of the surface beneath me; it is almost as if my body has become immune to the pain within my walls. I consider standing up, but as Angel Ariana lowers her arm down towards me, I know I must remain seated at her feet.

My body suddenly begins to tingle. The sensation runs across my shoulders and down my back. My guardian angel does not touch me, but I watch as a delicate stream of golden yellow light appears from the center of the palm of her hand. It pours out of her hand and travels directly down to my left shoulder where it rests. Angel Ariana does not speak. She doesn't need provide me with any instructions, as I feel an encouragement coming from the light to close my eyes.

As I allow my eyelids to slowly shut, the appearance of my angel is replaced with the presence of a most fantastic bright light. This light is not a golden colour like the light Angel Ariana projected down onto me; it is a much more powerful bright white light that seems to take over all of my senses.

My head becomes light on my shoulders. I start to become aware of changes around me. The damp scent of the thick air within my four walls has been replaced with a more striking assortment of aromas: the faint scent of burnt-out charcoal; a delicate heat of freshly baked bread; the bitter-fresh air of autumn.

A light breeze begins to wisp around me. It does not hurt me or cut into me, but I am aware of its chill as it nips lightly at my skin. The air around me is almost silent. In the distance, I can hear only a faint scratching, unsure of where this is coming from.

Angel Ariana asks me to concentrate on the white light. I watch it as it begins to grow in my mind. As I observe, I can see a figure beginning to form in its center. A woman is sitting at a small wooden table in the middle of a room. It looks like a kitchen, but the room is almost bare and tiny in size, with little to offer for a home. I focus on what the woman at the table is wearing. She is dressed in old-fashioned clothing; I struggle to work out when they are from, but accept that the woman is not from this century. I notice that her white shirt is a little dirty, and the bottom of her brown skirt is frayed from where she keeps standing on it. She has worn this outfit many times before. I find myself wondering if she owns any other clothes. She seems to be wearing a soft shawl of some sort. It is a slightly lighter shade than her skirt, and it is tied loosely around her neck to offer her warmth. It is stained, and there are little rips around the edges.

The woman is writing something as she leans over the table. I try to focus on the paper but I am unable to read what it says. Angel Ariana allows the vision to focus more closely, and I start to make everything out as the image becomes clearer. I am told to concentrate. I am about to be shown something very important.

Chapter Six

She lifted up the knife from the top of the kitchen table. Its handle had started to rust slightly, having been left in the damp drawer, but the blade was still sharp enough to function. She concentrated as she positioned the blade against the tip of the pencil. She struck the knife down, allowing the little wooden shavings to curl slightly. She repeated this all the way around until the pencil was sharpened enough for her to use it. Placing the tip of the pencil onto the thin sheet of paper in front of her, she paused for a second as she waited for the words.

Nothing came to her. She couldn't think of anything to write; no emotions came flooding to her, no notions arose to express her inner desires. Why was she finding this so difficult? She was sure it never used to be this much of a challenge. She was beginning to think she had lost all sense of who she was.

Over the years Fiona McGonnell had sprawled her name across the bottom of countless poems that she had scribbled onto scraps of paper and tatty notes. She would always take great care in shaping each letter with precision; she believed that the presentation of her work was just as important as the words she had chosen. Not that she could really call her writing *work*. She had never actually let anybody read anything that she had written. She knew she would never be able to get anything she wrote published, least of all because she was a woman, but Fiona didn't really think her words were good enough for the public eye anyway. She was proud of her collection, and loved the feeling that arose when she added a new completed poem to it, but she was sure her writing was never going to be to anybody else's taste. Instead, she kept her growing pile of poetry locked away inside a little metal tin, which she kept hidden away wrapped inside a blanket that she had folded over a few times to act as a cover to protect her writing. There they would be safe and out of sight.

She remained at the table, with her mind still void of all words. She was starting to feel anxious about something, but she couldn't quite put her finger on the cause of her growing apprehension. In the back of her mind she knew she should be worrying about something, but she had no idea what it was. Perhaps she had forgotten to pick something up from the village. She was sure she didn't have to be anywhere in the morning. Very rarely did she have any reason to leave the house, other than to fetch something from the grocer's or butcher's. She was sure whatever was bothering her would be realised later on. For now, she just wanted to release this unusual growing frustration on paper.

Eventually, she managed to scribble down a few words. They didn't really make any sense to her at that stage but it was a start. She was still lacking inspiration though. "I know what I need," she told herself in an attempt to regain her creativity. She pushed her chair backwards and stood up to walk through to her bedroom. It didn't take her very long, as the house consisted of only three rooms, and none of them were of any great size.

She approached the wooden chest that sat at the end of the bed. It groaned at her as she lifted its lid. She pulled out the blanket and placed it on the floor in front of her. Resting on her knees, she began to unravel it until she revealed the metal tin that was protected in the middle. She pushed the blanket to one side, and placed the tin on the floor in its place.

She eased open the lid to reveal a pile of papers on the inside. Some were covered in odd words and sentences, containing pieces of work Fiona had yet to finish. Others were flooded with completed pieces, each one written out in an elegant hand. On top of the pile lay a small hardback book.

Fiona lifted the book out and rested it in her lap. She stroked the hard cover for a second, admiring its colour. It had started to fade a little as it began to age, but it still reminded her of the dark cooling night sky. She allowed her fingers to become at one with the natural ridges of the hardback as she ran her hand across the spine.

Fiona took care in teasing the book open. She

turned to the page where she'd left her bookmark; between the pages that contained her favourite poem, she always kept a little note of paper that she had received with the book. It had been a present from a neighbour, given to her for her eighteenth birthday.

As a single parent raising his only daughter from her birth, William Fraser found that he was never able to bring in a lot of money for the household. Regardless of the fact that he often had to manage two jobs at once, he always seemed to struggle to rub enough money together to feed his young daughter. He made sure that Fiona never had to go without though; if it meant that he was unable to eat for days to ensure that she had enough food to keep her own health up then that was just the way it had to be. It often meant that his own health was in a poor state, and this was something he would often have to pay for, especially as I grew older.

William had been working in the Salmon Fisheries when his condition started to deteriorate. He had awoken one morning with a slight tickling sensation in his chest. It was no more than a mild inconvenience, he thought. He went off to work that day not bothering to think anything of it. While he was out, Fiona carried on with her own daily routine and knocked on the doors of her neighbours to seek out any extra work that was being offered.

Fiona had been fortunate enough to receive a few years of tutoring from the local teacher when she turned five years old. William didn't have a lot of money, but he was able to persuade Mr Benson to tutor Fiona with the agreement that William would manage his garden three times a week. It wasn't a particularly large garden, and William was sure that it didn't need to be seen to so frequently, but if he had to suffer constant backache at the hands of Mr Benson's assortment of plants so that Fiona could receive some education, then it was something he was prepared to do.

Despite the fact that Mr Benson had been quite strict in his approaches, Fiona had adored him. He taught her how to count, and how to write out the alphabet. He even gave her permission to look at the small map he carried around with him in his case. After she had finished her assigned task for the day, she would sit on the floor with her legs crossed in front of her tutor, listening intently to Mr Benson's stories about how he had traveled to lots of foreign countries and fascinating places. Fiona always dreamed of being able to see the world. How she longed to climb the Alps of Switzerland, or swim in Turkish waters, or eat lavish foods in the capital of France. As she grew older, Fiona often wondered how much truth was in Mr Benson's tales. He was a fantastic storyteller though; that was something she would always greatly give him credit for.

Mr Benson's anecdotes, however fictitious they may have been, had filled Fiona with a great passion for creating stories of her own. Unfortunately, though, her education from Mr Benson came to an abrupt end. Not long after her seventh birthday her father had to resign from his gardening duties. He had had no choice but to take up a second job that provided financial income for the family. It had broken his heart when he had to break the news to his daughter that she would no longer be able to continue with her numbers or with her reading, but he was left with no other option. Money was tighter than it had ever been before.

Fiona could still remember, quite clearly, the afternoon she had first spent with Mrs Lytton. She had been running around in the warm breeze, enjoying the new spring as she played amongst the trees. She was chasing a little butterfly that kept teasing her by fluttering away and coming back to her. She had been skipping along to catch the colourful creature and hadn't noticed the log that was stretched out ahead of her. Fiona caught the toe of her little shoe against the edge of the grubby log, which sent her flying onto the ground. She landed with a thud on top of a small pile of stones, which had inevitably decided to tear into her knee. They hadn't cut her skin too deeply, but the sight of the blood as it oozed rose-red out of her milky-white skin was enough to urge her into an attack of uncontrollable screaming.

Mrs Lytton lived in the small cottage on the corner of the street, just up from where Fiona and her father lived in Balgownie. She appeared at her front door to see what all of the commotion was about when she heard a small child crying. When she saw young Fiona clutching herself amongst the trees, Mrs Lytton had rushed over instinctively to make sure that she was not too badly hurt. She could tell that there was going to be no damage done to Fiona's poor knee, but she decided to carry the child into her house to clean her up and calm her down.

Fiona could only remember seeing Mrs Lytton on one occasion before that incident. She and her father had walked to the greengrocer's in the village to fetch the shopping for Mrs Lytton; the cold weather had affected the lady's hip, Fiona's father had explained, so they were going to collect her orders for her as she was having difficulties walking long distances in the snowy weather. Mrs Lytton had given them enough money to buy a few extra oranges for Fiona and her father to take for themselves. It was the best orange that Fiona had ever tasted.

As Fiona recalled this memory as she sniveled through the graze on her knee, she couldn't help but notice the way Mrs Lytton was now hobbling slightly as she carried her into her front room. She sat Fiona down on the edge of the chair. "You wait right here while I go and fetch something to clean up your wee knee," Mrs Lytton had told her before exiting into the kitchen.

Fiona was amazed at how comfortable the chair was. It was cushioned, soft; it wasn't anything at all like the hard furniture they had at home that left bruises on the back of her thighs whenever she sat down.

Mrs Lytton returned a few moments later, carrying with her a small bowl of water and a clean rag. She eased herself down onto the floor in front of Fiona, supporting herself with the arm of the chair as she moved onto her knees. She soaked the rag in the water before twisting it so that it was only a little damp. Fiona winced as she began to dab the cold water onto her cut.

"Don't worry, dear. This will only take a moment."

And Mrs Lytton was right. Before Fiona knew it, her knee had been cleaned up. The prickly pain had been taken away almost instantly with the dirt. She didn't know how Mrs Lytton had done it, but she was sure it had been some sort of magic. "Thank you," she whispered.

"You're very welcome. What were you doing in the woods anyway?"

"I was just playing, Miss. Father's been out working all day, and I get lonely if I sit in the house on my own."

"You call me Ma'am, dear, not Miss."

"Sorry, Ma'am. Nobody teaches me how to speak properly. I haven't been able to go to school since I was seven." There was a sadness in Fiona's voice.

"You haven't been to school since you were seven? And how old are you now?" Ms Lytton held onto the chair as she pulled herself up, holding the bowl of water in her free hand.

"I'm ten, Miss!" Fiona blushed when she realised her mistake. "Ma'am."

"Is that so? Well, why don't I make us something nice to eat, and you can tell me all about the games that you were playing among the trees before you fell over and hurt your poor knee?" Fiona's face lit up at the idea. She hated being lonely, forever having to spend time in her own company, and she couldn't remember the last time she had something proper to eat. "I won't be a moment."

Mrs Lytton carried the bowl of water back through to the kitchen. Fiona swung her legs lightly back and forth in her contentment. She cast her eyes around the room, taking in her surroundings. She decided that Mrs Lytton had a very lovely home. She noticed how warm it was; for once she didn't feel a need to hug her own body to stop herself from shivering. Mrs Lytton's home wasn't littered with furniture or too many ornaments, but Fiona decided that it displayed just the perfect amount to make it a comfortable environment. It was very neat and tidy, not at all dark or damp like the house she shared with her father.

A sweet scent began to drift through the air from the kitchen. Fiona twitched her nose as she inhaled the delight of the aroma. She watched as Mrs Lytton walked back into the living room, and placed a slightly worn silver tray on top of the table. She noticed Fiona's eyes widen with curiosity at the sight of the tea set that rested on top of the tray.

"It was my mother's," she explained, gesturing towards the crockery. "I was always fascinated by it myself when I was a little girl." Centered in the middle of the two fragile cups, each one sitting on its own matching saucer, there was a small teapot. Fiona followed the gold swirls of the patterns that decorated each item, admiring the way they created little flower shapes against the pastel pink backgrounds. She had never seen anything so pretty before.

"They're beautiful!" she exclaimed. She watched as Mrs Lytton picked up the teapot. As she held securely onto its lid to make sure it didn't fall off, she poured out the tea into the two cups. The excitement grew in Fiona as she watched Mrs Lytton spoon out a little sugar into each cup, before stirring it in with the tea. Fiona listened intently to the fascinating clinking sound the spoon made as it tickled against the sides of the china cups. She became almost mesmerised as she listened to it; she thought it was so delicate and calming, yet also loud and echoing at the same time. She'd heard nothing like it.

Mrs Lytton handed Fiona a little plate from the edge of the tray. Upon the plate sat two slices of thick white bread, one sitting on top of the other. Mrs Lytton had cut the bread twice down the middle to make four little square shapes for her guest. She had removed the crusts for her too. Fiona couldn't believe how thick the slices were. Her father would always ration a loaf of bread by cutting slices as thinly as he possibly could. He would do this until it could no longer be eaten, and even then they would sometimes have to risk consuming it, eating around the bits that looked a little fuzzy. They couldn't afford to just throw the bread away.

"You do like honey, don't you, Fiona?" Mrs Lytton questioned, picking up half of her own sandwich. She took a bite out of the side.

"I've never had honey before, Ma'am." Fiona sent her eyes down towards her plate. She felt a sense of embarrassment as she thought about how they didn't have enough money to have honey in the house.

"You've never had honey?" Ms Lytton noticed the look of shame that blushed to the surface of Fiona's cheeks. It was only then that she had properly paid attention to the rip in the side of Fiona's little red dress. She noticed the frayed crimson ribbon that she had tied into the back of her dark brown hair. Mrs Lytton wondered if the hole in the child's right shoe only came about when she had tripped in the woods. Her small fingernails, too, were thick with dirt. "Well, never mind," she continued. "You can try it now, and if you don't like it you don't have to eat it."

Fiona drew one of the little squares towards her lips and sniffed. Her mouth started to water at the thought of the fresh bread. She took a bite out of the sandwich, allowing it to sit in her mouth for a second so she could absorb the taste. She took another bite. And another. And then another. She chewed, trying to take in the full delicious flavour. She became amazed by the tingling sensation that coated her taste buds; she could definitely taste the sweetness of the honey, but decided that it had a surprisingly tangy sensation to it at the same time. The texture had taken her by surprise. The honey had begun to crystallise on the surface of the bread, presenting to Fiona a peculiarly delightful crispness within the softness of the runny honey. She could think of no food quite like it.

"What do you think?" Mrs Lytton asked with curiosity.

Fiona nodded with a smile. She chewed the mouthful before swallowing to reply. "It's delicious, thank you." Fiona proceeded to devour the remaining three squares of her honey sandwich, trying not to seem rude by shoveling it down as quickly as possible. She couldn't believe how wonderful it tasted.

After gulping down the last of the treat, she licked the sticky honey from her fingers. She decided that its bright golden colour was just as wondrous as its taste. Having satisfied her stomach with the meal, she turned her attention to her cup of tea.

"Careful, dear. It'll still be a bit hot," Mrs Lytton warned her, as she finished taking a sip from her own drink.

Fiona sat with the cup cradled in between her hands. She leaned forwards slightly to inhale the sugary warmth of the tea. She had tried tea once before, she remembered, as a treat for her birthday a few years ago, but she didn't think she would be tasting it again any time soon. She took a small sip, allowing the hot, sweet liquid to trickle down her throat. It instantly comforted her from the inside. She decided then that she felt very safe being in Mrs Lytton's home.

Fiona drained her tea cup and thanked Mrs Lytton for her kindness. "I really should be getting back home now, Mrs Lytton. My father should be on his way back from work, and he'll worry about me if I'm not there when he returns. Thank you for the food, and for the tea. I've had a lovely afternoon."

"It's been a pleasure, Fiona. And between you and me, I've appreciated the company! Hold on a second, dear. I just want to go and fetch something for you."

Fiona stood in the center of the front room, feeling a little out of place as she listened to Mrs Lytton climb the stairs. She noticed through the window that it had started to turn darker outside. Yet, somehow Mrs Lytton's house still seemed so bright and alert.

"Here you go. I knew it was still up there!" As Ms Lytton entered the front room again, she handed Fiona a small book. It couldn't have been any greater than twenty pages in length.

"What's this for?" Fiona questioned.

"I'd like you to read it. That is, if you want to. My own children used to enjoy this one a lot when they were your age. That was a long time ago now though, of course."

"I...I'm not sure if I will be able to," Fiona shuffled her feet, embarrassed. "Ma'am."

"Well why don't you take it with you and give it a go? If you find that you're struggling, if it's too difficult for you just now, you could bring it back and we can go through it together. How does that sound?"

"That sounds wonderful, Mrs Lytton. Thank you! You really don't mind?"

"Nonsense, dear. Of course I don't mind! It would only be lying around upstairs not doing anything. Somebody might as well put it to good use. I will need it back eventually, mind, but there's absolutely no rush for you to get it finished."

"Oh, thank you, thank you!" Out of nowhere, Fiona leapt forward and wrapped her arms around Mrs Lytton's waist. She hugged her tightly, overjoyed. She wondered what adventures she would discover inside the book. "I'll take good care of it, I promise!"

"I know you will, Fiona. You best run along now. You don't want to keep your father waiting. But please feel free to come by and visit me any time you like. I'm sure there will be more books where that one came from for you to explore."

Fiona pressed the book close to her chest to protect it as she walked down the front path. "Oh, I will come back very soon, Mrs Lytton. I promise! Thank you for the book, I can't wait to read it." She skipped along the street towards the little bridge that took her to her own house, having forgotten all about the cut on her knee, as Mrs Lytton watched her from the doorway. She followed Fiona with her eyes for a moment until she turned the corner out of sight. She thought about how long it had been since there were any children in her house. She had welcomed Fiona's spirited youth into her home with delight. It was so refreshing to have a child around her again. She hoped the young girl would visit again soon.

Mrs Lytton needn't have worried. Fiona visited her neighbour many more times over the years.

Fiona now carried the blue book into the

kitchen, and rested it on the top of the table. She crossed one leg over the other as she sat down and leaned forwards. She pressed the book open at where she had left the bookmark, her eyes barely glancing over the words as she began to read out the poem that was displayed at the top of the page. She paused as she turned the words of the first stanza of 'She Walks in Beauty' over in her mind. "*Starry skies.* Isn't that such a beautiful image?" There was nobody around to hear her speaking out loud. "The contrast of the bright stars against the blackness of the night sky is so wonderful, so powerful," she thought to herself. "It's untouchable, yet so real at the same time."

Fiona had memorised the poem many years ago. She always found great comfort in its words. After she'd borrowed the small children's book from Mrs Lytton, she had to confess to her that she had found the simple narrative quite challenging to read. She had expressed her embarrassment in this, but Mrs Lytton assured her that it was nothing to be ashamed about. She offered to teach Fiona how to read in return for her company.

Just as Mrs Lytton had hoped, Fiona had jumped at the opportunity, and soon found herself spending countless days in the warmth of her neighbour's home. They would sip cups of tea together and nibble on sweet biscuits as they devoured great stories and adventures.

As a special treat, Mrs Lytton would read out poetry to Fiona. Some of the poems she recited had been written by Mrs Lytton herself, but lots of them were works by those she described as history's most cherished writers. From the moment Fiona first heard the poem now in front of her, she had fallen in love with it.

"Before my husband Alfie and I began to court, he used to recite this poem to me," Mrs Lytton explained. "As soon as he spoke the beautiful lines with his gentle voice, I knew he was the one for me." Just as the lyric reminded Mrs Lytton of her husband, it soon became the poem that would make Fiona think of her dear neighbour.

She was taken completely by surprise when Mrs Lytton handed Fiona a small parcel wrapped in brown paper on the day of her eighteenth birthday. Mrs Lytton had been quite unwell in the months that led up to the day, and Fiona certainly hadn't expected her to find the energy to remember about her birthday, so the gift came as a complete surprise when Fiona went to visit Mrs Lytton to help around the house.

She received the parcel with curiosity. She tugged at the little thread that was holding the paper together to reveal the gift, and when she saw what was inside she gasped, shocked and delighted. Protected under the paper was the blue hardback book which was now sitting in front of her on the kitchen table. She had admired the collection of Lord Byron's poetry for many years, ever since she was a little girl when Mrs Lytton had first read her favourite poem from it. Fiona spent hours in her teenage years pouring her soul into the love-soaked stanzas as she performed some of them for Mrs Lytton. "It was given to me for *my* eighteenth birthday," Ms Lytton had explained to Fiona as she picked the book up from inside the paper. "I want you to have it now. I think you'll be able to give it a new loving home."

Over the last two years Fiona had spent

countless hours devouring Byron's words, engulfed by his adventures and breaking her heart over his own emotions. She found enjoyment in the story of Childe Harold, and couldn't help but admire the creativity that went into *Don Juan*, but she found that her own passions were echoed in the poet's own prolific personality that he so honestly expressed in his shorter lyrics. Fiona felt that he was dark and daring, but also that he must have been a very kind soul. It was inevitable that she, like many others before her, was going to be drawn to this sensational man from such a young age.

She finished reading the poem for the countless time, and sat with the last words in her mind for a few moments before turning her attention to the piece of paper in front of her. She scribbled a few words down, little more than the first things that came into her head. "I don't think Lord Byron would think much of my writing! His own words are so perfectly arranged, so moving. They paint such vivid pictures. My words just seem to be scattered about with no real connection," she sighed to herself, adding a final line to the draft of her poem. It would have to do for now. Maybe she could revise it later when she was feeling more inspired.

She leaned back in her chair and stared blankly into the air. "My dearest Lord Byron, what has happened to my words? They seem to have run off and abandoned me all on my own." A single tear rolled down her cheek as she tried to reach out for the feelings that had long escaped her. "I try to find it deep inside, to see if I can locate where it's hiding, but...nothing." She tried to search for an answer to her own question. She was beginning to wonder if there was ever anything there. Perhaps she had just been fooling herself. Maybe her heart didn't beat as she thought it did.

Fiona shoved the piece of paper inside the poetry book and closed it shut. "My father would be so disappointed in me. He always thought I'd be an appreciated writer. And what ever would Mrs Lytton think?!" Her thoughts were sad as she allowed herself to become lost in her memories, addressing nobody in particular any more. "If it wasn't for her, I probably wouldn't have even remembered how to write my own name. She invested so much in me. Where did I go wrong?"

Noticing a breeze in the room, she turned her attention away from the table and reached to shut the kitchen window. She opened the cupboard door and lifted out a candlestick and a small packet of matches. She placed the candlestick on the table and proceeded to light the candle. It had already melted down to half of its original size. Making sure the poetry book wasn't anywhere near the candle in case any drips of wax were to fall down onto it, Fiona struck a match and held it next to the wick for a moment. The little flame began to dance as it came to life.

She turned her back to the candle to face the window, allowing the soft glow of the candle light to float around the room as she stared out into the night sky. She couldn't begin to imagine how many hours she had spent gazing out of that very window in the exact same way as she was doing now as she waited for her father to return from work. She found the experience to be relaxing, the light of the evening moon providing a comfort to her loneliness. She looked up and counted the stars in the sky. Out of the corner of her eye, she noticed the front door handle slowly turn. She faced away from the window in time to watch as his silhouette emerged out of the darkness.

Chapter Seven

I can feel Angel Ariana's energy leaving me as she lifts her hand back down to her side. Before she goes she tells me that I must keep the image I've just witnessed in my head. It's important that I don't forget it. She will be back soon, but for now she must leave.

I'm all alone again.

I sit with my eyes closed for a moment, not wanting to open them to the darkness that has once again fallen into my walls. I don't know what I am supposed to feel any more. In the presence of my guardian angel I know I felt safe. I was sure nothing would be able to hurt me. But now I'm confused, not sure of anything. Why did she show me this woman?

I search for the image and play it over again inside my mind. In the pit of my stomach, I can still feel her hunger. She was aching, and yet the woman didn't appear to show any anguish over her condition. It was something she was used to. She looked so thin, so weak. There was such sadness behind her eyes. She was hurting inside, I could feel it. My own heart pulls as I witness her tears.

I was being opened up to the suffering felt by this woman. She was dressed so poorly. Her clothes were filthy; the dull colours appeared to be covered in stains that I couldn't begin to count. And yet she still managed to look so beautiful. There was a gentle smile on her face. It was as if her suffering was unable to reach into her soul, only penetrating her earthly existence. Her cheekbones were hollow, the wisps of her dark brown hair curling around her face as they highlighted her naturally pretty features. I can feel the kindness in her heart.

I am overcome with compassion for this woman as I think about her. I still don't know what I am supposed to do with this though. A single tear rolls down my cheek as I continue to feel the suffering. I hope Angel Ariana will return soon to enlighten me.

I open my eyes and wipe them dry. I suddenly become aware of the cold, hard surface beneath me again. There is nobody in here to protect me from it any more. The thickness of the air is starting to suffocate me again. I inhale the dust once more. I cough as I feel it coating my lungs, spreading a line across the inside of my stomach as it makes its way further inside me. The pressure within my walls increases. The air becomes even heavier, making it more difficult to breathe. I start to panic as it becomes darker, the walls rebelling against my own quest for light.

I want to get out of here. I want to escape. But

he's out there. I know he is. I cannot leave. If I do, he'll be able to get to me. He'll be able to hurt me. He will crush me. I am safer in here, safer in the darkness. But he is trying to get to me. I can feel it. I pull my legs into my chest again and hug onto my knees. The ground is cold and damp, but it is safer in here than it is out there.

He cannot touch me in here. He cannot harm me. He cannot kill me.

Chapter Eight

The glass clinked against the bottle as Peter poured the last of the wine out. He only acknowledged that he had emptied the bottle as he watched the last few drops drip into his glass. They splashed as they met with the surface of the drink. He slammed the bottle down on the top of the table, annoyed. Peter refused to blame himself for the fact that the bottle was finished. He would never admit that he was in the wrong, no matter what the situation.

Maggie could see the empty bottle out of the corner of her eye. She was relieved that it was all gone, even if it did mean that Peter had drunk an incredible amount more than he could cope with. At least he wouldn't be able to drink any more that night. She knew that it would still take a while for the effects of the full quantity of the wine to kick in though.

It was actually quite rare to find that there was no more alcohol in the house. Peter usually kept wine or vodka in the cupboard, and occasionally whisky if he was going through one of his infrequent phases where he would tire of drinking the same thing. There was little that Peter wouldn't drink.

Maggie had often thought about hiding his alcohol when he was out at work. She never found the strength to do so though; she knew it would only make situations worse. Maggie reminded herself that at least when Peter was drunk his aim was a little off. He never missed her when he was sober.

She was standing by the kitchen door now. She had managed to support herself through her increasing exhaustion by leaning against the door frame. She longed to sit down, but she knew that if she did so she would become more vulnerable to her husband. This way, he had less of a chance to look down on her.

Her legs ached, and the top of her arm pulsed slightly as she leaned against it. She was thankful that the bruising down her back was hurting a little less now though, but she found that she was starting to suffer from a growing headache. She hoped it wouldn't progress into a migraine, but she knew it was only going to get worse if she didn't go to bed soon.

"Do you mind if I go for a lie down, Peter?"

"Why would you want to do that?" Peter had lost all sense of time. It didn't occur to him that it was now after eleven o'clock.

"I'm just feeling a bit of a headache coming on," Maggie tried to explain. She wanted to get away from Peter. "I won't be..."

"No."

"No?" she took a step back into the kitchen as Peter stepped away from the table and walked towards her. The liquid in his glass swirling around, splashing as he staggered slightly.

"That's what I said, wasn't it? I'm hungry. You," he jabbed her in the chest, "need to be a good little wife and make me something to eat." The force of his finger left a painful red mark on Maggie's skin.

Maggie knew better than to argue with Peter when he had had this much to drink. If she just gave into his demands, she would hopefully be able to go to bed afterwards. Plus, giving him something to eat would help to sober him up.

She took a deep breath as she fought her way through the headache. "Okay, Peter. What do you want?" He followed her further into the kitchen. Maggie turned her attention to the fridge as she opened the door. "I could cook you some sardines if you like? Or there's some cold pasta..."

"Bacon." Peter's face was uncomfortably close to Maggie's as he peered into the fridge to examine its contents. He reached in with a clumsy hand and grabbed hold of an unopened packet of bacon. "Here," he thrust the packet towards Maggie. She grabbed hold of it before it managed to fall down to the floor. "I want the lot."

"Are you sure, Peter? It's a full packet, you know. It hasn't been opened yet."

"Just cook the bacon, for goodness sake!"

Peter, clutching onto his half-empty glass, leaned on the frame of the kitchen door. He watched as Maggie fumbled around with the packet of meat. She struggled to open it, unable to concentrate or think clearly.

After a few moments of observing her tug at the plastic packet, Peter was becoming agitated. "Use the scissors, you stupid bloody woman!" His words were rushed, sharp.

Obeying, Maggie reached into the drawer next to the cooker and pulled out a pair of scissors. Trying to ignore Peter as he stood hovering behind her, she sliced the scissors through the plastic wrapping. She felt weak, pathetic. No wonder Peter was ashamed of her.

After Maggie had turned on the grill, the small kitchen began to feel a lot warmer. Under the glaring eyes of Peter, Maggie placed each slice of bacon onto the tray before sliding it under the grill. She made sure that every last strip was used, fearing that Peter would grow annoyed if he didn't get his full plate of meat.

She kept her back turned to him the whole time. The room was silent for a second, and then Peter snorted.

Maggie didn't turn around at the noise, so Peter decided to snort again. This time, Maggie summoned her energy to turn and face him.

"They're funny-looking, aren't they? Pigs."

It certainly wasn't what Maggie had expected Peter to come out with. "I suppose they are, yes." She folded her arms and rested herself against the counter opposite Peter. She was pleased that he was starting to slip into a talkative mood.

"I mean they start out all small and cute and squeaky, and then they turn into these... these..." He stretched his arms as far as they would go, not taking care of the wine that splashed in his glass as he clutched onto it. "They're huge! Massive pigs, they are! And what are they even good for? Nothing, I tell you. Nothing!"

"I'm sure that's not entirely true."

"Of course it is! It's the same with all animals. They just get in the way all the time."

Maggie pulled out the tray from beneath the grill. She turned the bacon over to cook on the other side, before sliding the tray back in.

"When I was a boy I had this German Shepherd," Peter began the story that Maggie had heard a million times over. "His name was Duck. Duck the dog, you know. I thought it was a good name at the time. Clever. Anyway, I loved Duck. One day, when I came home from school, my mother told me that Duck had been sent away. The usual cute story about how pets go off to a farm where they could play with all the sheep and the pigs and the...and the..." Peter thought to himself, and then smiled, amused. "And the ducks. But she lied, Margaret. Duck didn't go off to the farm. He was hit by a bus that morning. He never made it. Why didn't she just tell me the truth?" He finished the last of the wine from his glass and stumbled towards Maggie. He stood there for a second with his arms pressed into the counter either side of her. "I hate lies, Margaret. I hate them." There was almost a whimper of sadness in his voice, but the strong odour of alcohol didn't allow Maggie to feel any sympathy.

"Excuse me, Peter. I need to check the bacon." She nudged him out of the way so that he staggered slightly to her side. He returned to hovering over her shoulder as she turned off the grill. She proceeded to serve Peter's food on a plate she'd taken out of the cupboard. He stood behind her and tried to place his hands on her waist. Maggie recoiled as he touched her. Had he forgotten what he'd done? Couldn't he see the pain in her cheeks, the ache in her heart? She realised the second after the thoughts had run through her mind that, no, he probably couldn't. It wasn't even worth her trying to work out how much he'd had to drink, or what effect it would be having on his memory.

She turned around quickly and handed the plate to Peter. "Thanks," he grunted, before shuffling back into the living room and slouching into the sofa. "You know who I like?" he continued, chewing on a piece of bacon. "That woman. What's her name?"

"Who, Peter?" It took all of Maggie's energy to fake an interest in Peter's drivel as she sat back in her own chair. She leaning herself sleepily on her left side.

"You know, the one with the curves. The brunette woman. From that TV show." Peter shoveled down the last few strips of bacon and let the plate drop down to the floor. "It could have been doing with some sauce, but whatever." He sank further back into the sofa. He closed his eyes for a moment, silent.

Maggie allowed her own eyes to close, hoping to drift off into the comforts of a dream that could take her far away. Peter would hopefully start to sober up now; it usually didn't take him too long to do so after he had something to eat. She winced as she rearranged the position of her legs to curl them beneath her, the bruise on her side letting her know that it was still there.

"Oh, I can't remember her name! You know who I'm on about though."

Peter's sudden demand for conversation alerted

Maggie, who had begun to fall asleep in the chair during the few minutes Peter had been silent. She opened her eyes to find that he had raised himself out of the sofa, and was now standing right in front of her. "Who, Peter?" She yawned, attempting to wake up a little.

"The woman from that bloody television programme! Keep up, will you? The chef woman. She knows where her place is, she does. She does all the cooking, without even being asked. And because she *knows* that that's her job, she puts the effort in and she does it well. Seriously, Margaret, only you could mess up bacon. Why can't you be more like her?"

"But you..." Maggie glanced at the empty plate that was still sitting abandoned on the floor. She didn't bother to continue her sentence. She knew it wouldn't matter to Peter that he had eaten the entire plateful. She stretched herself out of the chair and forced her energy across to pick up the greasy plate. She placed it in the kitchen sink where she would have to face it again in the morning. She was sure she could think of a better way to start the day than by tackling Peter's dirty dishes, but there wasn't any point. Her routine was never going to change.

Peter, having vanished into the bedroom at the same time that Maggie went into the kitchen, now emerged back into the frame of the living room door. He started pushing his left arm into the sleeve of his leather jacket.

Maggie stared at him for a moment, before being able to speak. "Where are you going?"

"Out." He ruffled up his hair with his hands, attempting to make himself more presentable. It didn't make a difference.

"Where, Peter? Do you know what time it..."

"I'm going to the off-license, if you must know. I won't be long."

"Oh, Peter, please don't. Look, why don't I make us both a cup of coffee and we can..."

"Have you seen my wallet?" He reached a hand into the back of his trouser pocket and pulled out what he was looking for, not paying attention to what Maggie was suggesting. He opened it to see how much money was inside. "That should be enough," he announced, before striding his way towards the front door. Maggie noticed he had to reach for the door handle twice before being able to grab hold of it.

"Peter, please. Peter! Don't buy anything! Peter, wait!" Maggie tried to call after him, but it was too late. He was gone, slamming the front door shut as he left. She forced herself through to the living room. She allowed herself to fall back in the chair, giving in to her lack of energy.

He was going to come back with another bottle of wine, she knew it. She needed to go to bed before he started drinking any more. She was devastated. She had been certain that he was going to start sobering up once he had had something to eat. She felt like a fool for having ever thought it. Pressing her own arms against the arms of the chair, she lifted herself out and made her way through to the bedroom.

She had tried to avoid it, but she couldn't. There it stood, staring at her. Her own reflection. The mirror stood towering and powerful, forcing her to stare back at her own image that was presented before her. Through the natural darkness of the room, Maggie could see that her make up was a mess. Tiny parallel tracks of black mascara had trickled down her cheeks as her tears had raced one another. Her hair looked as if it hadn't seen a brush in weeks. Exhausted, she decided that she didn't have the energy to do anything about it just now. She would still look a mess in the morning.

Sitting down on the edge of the bed, she slipped off her tights and dropped them in a small pile on the floor in front of her. The cold air of the bedroom would normally be a cause for her to dive right under the bed covers, but tonight she found it refreshing. It was a comfort to her. She remained still for a moment, staring into the space in front of her. She thought about nothing in particular as she concentrated on the cool draft.

The front door banged shut, causing Maggie to jump out of her daze with fright. She listened as a pair of heavy boots stamped their way through the hall and into the living room. A weak cough sounded, followed by a few mumbles and a grunt. She needed to lie down while she had the chance.

"Margaret!"

It was too late. She couldn't move. She didn't have the strength to creep under the covers, nor could she find the energy to obey the call. Maggie remained perched on the end of the bed.

"Margaret, get in here!"

She couldn't escape the tone in Peter's voice. It would only make the situation worse. She managed to pad her way out of the bedroom, the wooden flooring of the hallway sending a chill through her as her bare feet forced their way across it into the living room. Her heart paused as her eyes locked onto the object that now sat on the table.

"I thought you were going to buy more wine?"

Peter was resting against the table, his jacket hanging carelessly over the back of the wooden chair. Maggie guessed that it was raining outside, as little drops of water sat on the shiny surface of the leather. "Nope. Never said that, never intended that." He ran his hand through his hair to shake off the rain.

The screw cap from the bottle had already been opened. The bright red colour sat glaring at Maggie, threatening her. She couldn't help but notice that some of the vodka was already missing. It didn't take her a second to realise that it was in the glass that Peter had wrapped his fist around tightly. He lifted it to his mouth and gulped down the drink.

Maggie didn't know what to say. In the moment, she decided that the safest thing for her to do would be to go along with him. "I think we have some lemonade you could add to it," she began as she turned towards the kitchen.

"Don't bother." He drained the glass, before filling it again, this time adding a little more than before. Maggie wanted to question why he was even bothering to use a glass, but she knew better than to give him any ideas to just drink it straight out of the bottle. The thought of the pure liquid running down her throat made her want to throw up. She didn't know how anybody could drink it without using a soft drink to dilute it first.

She needed to sit down. It was her turn to occupy the sofa. Unlike Peter, however, who liked to spread his entire body out across two cushions, Maggie sat herself in the corner of the seat, curling herself so that she barely required one cushion.

Peter began to pace the room, his boots loud against the floor. Not looking at Maggie, he spoke his thoughts. "Why do we bother?"

Confused, Maggie forced herself to look up at him. "Bother with what, Peter?"

"This. That. Everything." He lightly tapped the end of his boot against the skirting board beneath the window. He parted the blinds slightly with his free hand so that he could look out across the street. The area was lit up by a few weak street lamps that worked only when they decided that they wanted to.

Even if Maggie had any idea what Peter was going on about, she was sure it wouldn't make any difference to him. "I don't know Peter, maybe we just do," was all that she could reply.

"That's it though, isn't it?" He took a sip from his glass. "We just do. There's no point to our existence, is there?"

She couldn't be bothered to argue with Peter. She didn't agree with him – she was sure there was a purpose to life, even if she wasn't quite she what that purpose was - but sometimes it was best if she pretended that she did agree to keep her husband happy. "No, Peter. There is no point."

"I mean, take this piece of junk, for example." He plucked a small ornament up from the cabinet where it sat next to the sofa. He held it in the air between two fingers. It had been given to Maggie by her mother as a gift for her birthday a few years ago. The little grey teddy bear sat peacefully as it clutched onto a small green parcel with a yellow ribbon. There was a banner wrapped around the base that read *Happy Birthday!* in bold pink lettering. Little pictures of balloons could be seen at either side to add colour to the display. Maggie had thought that the teddy bear looked rather cute, with its wide eyes and its dainty little nose. "Can you imagine what was going through the guy's head that created this?! I mean, what was he thinking? 'I know what we need! Little bears that do nothing but sit on a shelf looking stupid and gather dust!'" he mocked. "I just don't get it." He let the ornament slip out of his fingers.

Maggie watched, her own eyes wide, as it plummeted to the floor. As it collided with the hard flooring, she heard a crack as the teddy bear's fragile little head landed awkwardly and detached from the rest of its body. She stared for a moment, unable to work out what had just happened, before turning to Peter. "What...why?" was all she could manage.

"You don't need it," was all he had to say. "And this," he began as he stormed over to the table, turning his attention to the glass bowl that was always on display in the middle. "*This* serves no purpose either." He picked up the cream pillar candle from its dish. "You do realise that we are living in the twenty-first century, don't you, Margaret? We have electricity! I don't go out to work all day just so you can waste my money on stupid bloody candles!"

Maggie didn't say anything. She couldn't. She knew it would only infuriate him further. For as long as she could remember, she had loved to burn candles. She would have one burning throughout the day to keep her company; in the evening she would light one to help relax her. She wished she could stare into the calming light of a dancing flame at that moment. Instead, she averted her eyes away from Peter and stared at the candle in his hand.

"You know what I think of this, Margaret? You know what I think of your stupid candle?" She watched, startled, as Peter launched the candle out of his grasp. She tried not to gasp as it flew, soaring through the air. It bounced off of the wall at the other side of the room and fell onto the floor in front of the chair. It no longer represented a beautiful cylinder, but now a dinted mess. The impact had caused some of its scent to drift around the room, but even the sweetness of its delicate vanilla scent wasn't going to be enough to diffuse the situation.

Peter kicked the wooden chair out of the way of the table. Reaching into the bowl, he fished out a handful of smooth pebbles that were swimming in the water around the dish where the candle previously sat. His mind was empty for a moment as he felt the shiny wetness of the stones in his hand. Almost out of nowhere, he decided to aimlessly scatter them across the table. They clattered painfully as each one clashed with the wooden surface. Peter didn't notice that he was splashing water onto Maggie's scrapbook from where it remained ignored on top of the table. Not that he would have cared at all.

"You're pathetic."

Maggie drew herself inwards, not rising to his words. She kept her eyes to the ground.

"I mean it, Margaret. You're pathetic. *Pa – the – tic.*" He spat the words out at her as he stumbled his way towards her. He stopped in front of her before nudging her bare leg with the side of his dirty boot, the same way he had treated the skirting board a few moments before. "Get up."

Maggie heard Peter speak, but she was unable to acknowledge his words.

"Get up, Margaret! Don't be so bloody lazy. Move!"

She remained still, silent, not looking at Peter.

She hoped that he wouldn't notice the tears that were trickling down her face.

"Don't ignore me, you stupid bitch!" His voice was raised. Fear was sent running through Maggie as she felt the force of his words within her. She knew she had to listen to him. If she could only find the strength.

"I told you to get up!" He bellowed out the final note, belting the toe of his boot full force into her shin. This caused Maggie to shoot up as she tried not to scream from the pain that now took over all of her senses.

Satisfied with his work, Peter walked back over to the table and reached for his drink. Maggie forced herself to hobble through the pain as she tried to tidy up the damage. She placed the broken little teddy bear back on the top of the unit where he came from before he had been subjected to the violence. She had loved that ornament. She just had to remind herself that it was just that: an ornament. It was a material object that didn't add any real value to her life.

"Leave it." Peter ordered as Maggie was about to reach for the mess that had become of the candle. She didn't turn to look at him, but just stood there, frozen to the spot. She felt helpless. What was she to do? She didn't dare try and sit down again; the ache in her shin was a reminder of what cost that would bring to her.

There was an unexpected knock at the door. The three little raps were faint, very quiet, but they had both heard them.

Peter's head turned suddenly at the sound. "Who's that? Margaret? Who's at the door?"

"I don't know," she managed to whisper. How could she possibly be able to tell who it was?

"Just ignore it then. They should have a bit of respect, knocking on somebody's door at this time of night! Whoever it is can just go away."

The knocks sounded again, slightly louder this time. A little voice drifted through the letterbox. "Maggie, are you in there? It's me, Sharon."

"Sharon? What does she want?!"

"Maggie?" she asked again.

"Oh, for crying out loud, she's not going to shut up, is she? Stay there, don't move. I'll go." Peter ordered as he stumbled his way through the hall, leaving Maggie alone and motionless in the living room. "Sharon," he stated as he opened the door. His voice had sounded louder than he'd actually intended.

In front of him stood a woman who looked to be in her early sixties. She was no taller than five foot one in height, and stood wrapped in a floral pink nightgown. She had lived in the flat upstairs for more years than she could remember. She was there when had Maggie moved in with Peter.

Sharon took a step back from the door, partly out of shock, and partly to distance herself from the stench of alcohol that hit her in the face the moment Peter spoke. "Oh, hello, Peter. I was just finishing my book in bed," she spoke softly.

"So?"

"It's just that I thought I heard somebody shouting. I just wanted to make sure that everything was okay. I thought there might have been a...a burglar or something," she lied.

"So you came all the way downstairs to see if there was a burglar? What if somebody *was* trying to break in, Sharon? It would have been pretty foolish of you to risk your life like that, don't you agree?" Peter smirked. He had never liked this nosy bat.

"Yes, yes, I suppose it would have been. Sorry to bother you Peter." Shaking slightly, Sharon turned to walk back up to her own flat.

"You must just be tired, Sharon. Go to bed, you're hearing things!"

"Yes, Peter. Thank you, Peter," she stammered a response before starting back up the stairs.

Peter slammed the door shut and stormed back into the living room. "It was old Sharon from upstairs. She thought somebody was trying to break in! What a silly cow."

Maggie hadn't moved from where Peter left her. She stood, rooted to the carpet, too afraid to sit down. She had started to rock back and forth slightly, swaying in her own fear. She struggled to focus properly on her surroundings. She could hear Peter chuckle as he insulted their neighbour. It was a snarled laugh, evil in its tones. A second later, she felt him grab tightly onto of her right wrist.

"This is all *your* fault!" he whispered viciously into her ear. He twisted her arm slightly as he pushed her against the wall, before standing right in front of her. He cupped her face with his hands as he leaned into her, forcing her back against the radiator again. The strong pressure against the surface of her already-bruised back sent a roaring pain straight through her. She bit the inside of her lip to try and mask the ache as it grew unbearable.

His face was remarkably close to hers as he held onto the sides of her jaw. "You need to stop being such an idiot, Margaret," he breathed, smothering her with the horrid reek of vodka. He began turning her earrings around, twisting and tugging at them. Maggie tried to control her breathing as her heart raced. She was sure he was going to tear her earrings out straight through her ears. "You used to have such a pretty face."

Peter released his grip from her jaw, allowing Maggie a quick second to turn her head away from his. His nose was almost touching hers, threatening her. Instead of letting go of her, which Maggie had begun to foolishly hope that he would do, he forced her to inhale sharply as the shock of Peter dragging the jagged edges of his bitten finger nails down the bare flesh of her arms became an agony that was all too real. He moved his hands slowly, each finger working as a blade of torture cutting into her. He pushed her arms forcefully into the wall behind her as his nails bullied their marks into her pale skin.

He didn't say anything, but a sinister grin had stretched right across his face. His teeth were gritted as he concentrated. As he reached the bottom of her arms, Peter made sure he took extra care in digging his nails into the backs of Maggie's hands. The pain became unbearable. She couldn't hold it in any longer.

She screamed.

Peter flung his hand through the air and slapped her hard across the face. He wasn't satisfied with striking her just once. "Shut up! Shut up! Shut up!" With each demand he delivered a blow, before stepping back and allowing Maggie to slump to the floor. She arched herself around her knees, wrapping her arms around her bare legs as she cried uncontrollably, shaking.

Peter would usually order her to stop her crying, but on this occasion he found that he didn't say anything. Instead, he turned his back to her and rested his weight on his arms as he leaned against the table. He drained his glass of vodka, spluttering as he swallowed the last mouthful, before pouring more out. He only filled the glass halfway to the top this time, though he wasn't sure why. He supposed he could add more later on once he had finished drinking what he had served for himself.

He suddenly noticed the scrapbook lying there, having forgotten about it. He pulled it towards him to distract himself from Maggie's sobbing, not caring that it dragged across the water he'd splashed from the bowl of pebbles. He flipped over a few pages aimlessly until the book fell open at a sheet of sky blue card. In the center of the display lay a photograph. When Peter's eyes locked on it, it forced his concentration to snap back. He looked down at the picture. It was a photograph that he hadn't seen in years.

"The boy."

Chapter Nine

I can hear it. I can feel it. It's vibrating all around me. I pull myself up and walk across the room, cautious as I move through the darkness, taking care not to cut my bare feet on the broken shards. I lean forward and rest my body against the wall opposite from where I'd been sitting. I can see so little in the blackness, but the firm surface of the brick is a surprising comfort. It is real, it is there.

I press my right hand flat against the wall as I manoeuvre myself to rest on my left shoulder. The whole wall feels as though it's shaking. The air in the room is still, silent, but the wall... I can feel it, battling as it tries to move. I lean in closer, pressing my ear against the cool surface. The sound from the outside is muffled; it's faint, but it's there.

I'm unable to make out any of what's being said.

But I know he's shouting. He is always shouting. His voice bellows, echoing all around the space outside. I remain still for a moment, exhausted. I allow the breeze of the air to circulate around me, enveloping me in its soothing coolness. I turn around to support my back against the wall. I close my eyes, longing for sleep.

I breathe deeply. Inhale. Exhale. The chill of the cold air dives up my nostrils. It runs down my throat, awakening me from within. As I take in a sharp breath of air, I wince in pain. Every part of me aches. If only I could lie down, in my own bed, and wrap myself up in layers of soft, warm sheets.

Can you smell that? Through the air there is a scent. The sweet aroma is almost sugary. What is it? It's such a delicate smell, so soft and lovely. It reminds me of butter cream, or perhaps vanilla icing. The delicious kind you find wedged in the middle of birthday cakes that fills you with an exciting rush of sickly energy. I allow it to take over my senses, coating them in its warmth.

A white light begins to emerge behind my eyelids. I snap my eyes open, startled. I can see her again; she is standing in front of me, little more than a meter away in the very spot upon which I was sitting previously.

I step an inch away from the wall. Now that I'm no longer on the ground but standing upright, I can see that she is only a little taller than I am, perhaps by a few inches or so, but she appears to be slightly more slender in frame. My guardian angel looks almost human – the dainty features of her face are not too dissimilar to those of my own – but the sense that there's something about her which tells me that she is so much more divine than any earthly existence is heightened now that I find myself standing directly in front of her. She glows still, and the wings that cascade down her back appear more full of life than they were before. I'm sure they've grown longer too.

Unexpectedly, I find the courage within me to ask Angel Ariana why she is here. She does not answer me, but instead she looks directly into my eyes. Her own eyes twinkle at me. I watch as a faint silver light grows around her middle. It circles, creating a belt of light around her waist. It seems to accentuate the beauty of her dress, and that of her own self.

The light grows from around her waist and starts moving towards me. It creates a sort of path as it grows closer. It looks at first like a simple beam of light, but I notice that it appears to be moving from within itself. It reminds me of a river as it makes its way down its stream. It starts to pick up pace as it flows in my direction from Angel Ariana.

The river of light merges with my own stomach. As it touches me, my whole body begins to tingle. The sensation feels similar to those experienced with pins and needles, but more gentle. Angel Ariana is smiling at me. It's a smile that I know is full of care and compassion. I feel safe with my guardian angel in front of me.

As I listen, I'm no longer able to hear the noise from outside my walls. The space around me still lies in complete darkness. I concentrate on the shimmering form that connects me with Angel Ariana.

I close my eyes upon her request. Though I am unable to see her, I know that my guardian angel is still with me, as the strong light behind my eyelids remains. Every fiber in my body continues to tingle. It doesn't hurt, but is instead very peaceful. I feel weightless, as if I'm floating high on a cloud, away from all the chaos of everyday life. My body is warm, but around my feet I can feel a peculiar breeze that makes me curious. Angel Ariana asks me to focus on this sensation. As I do so, my head begins to clear, as if my mind is drifting outside of my body.

The bright light starts to fade, and is replaced with the image of the kitchen that I was previously asked to observe. As I focus on this once more, I can see the same woman who was in the room before. She is sitting down at the table again, but this time she isn't alone.

Chapter Ten

Fiona pulled her chair in closer towards the table and looked down at her plate. Martin was sitting in the chair to the side of her, concentrating as he tore into a slice of bread and butter. Fiona watched as he pulled apart the crust before shoveling it into his mouth, barely taking a moment to chew the food before swallowing it. The hard crumbs scattered noisily as they fell down onto the plate in front of him.

Martin lifted up his head to face Fiona as he finished the last of his supper. "Thank you," he muffled with a mouthful of bread. "I've felt famished all afternoon at work." He stretched his tongue out to lick a smudge of butter that had decided to rest itself on the side of his lip.

Fiona picked up her own supper and began to nibble at its edges. She didn't really feel like eating on that particular evening, but she decided that she must try something for she had not had the desire to eat anything since the morning. "Did you have a good day?" She didn't look at Martin as she spoke, but instead kept her eyes on her own plate.

"It was fairly tolerable. This afternoon John dropped a barrel of fish all over the floor so the master wasn't exactly happy with him. The rest of us felt the end of it too, of course, but the poor kid's only been there for a few months. I'm sure he's going to be told to leave soon."

Martin had worked with Fiona's father in the fish processing business ever since Fiona was just a young teenager. Martin had been no more than nineteen years of age himself when William had introduced him to his only daughter. William had known that his health was deteriorating; his time was running out, he was painfully aware of that, and he hated the thought of leaving Fiona all on her own after he had gone. They didn't have any family left and, regardless of the fact that she was surely old enough to look after herself, as she kept reminding him, William worried that the loneliness would drive Fiona insane. She was rarely presented with the opportunity to socialise with anybody, and it would only become a more infrequent happening once William was no longer with her. She would struggle greatly to find a husband, he knew.

He had sat down with Fiona one evening and explained to her, his daughter then of sixteen years, that he had found a lovely young man for her who he thought would be able to take good care of her. Having spent most of her years on her own during the many hours when her father had to be out at work, Fiona's eyes lit up at the thought of having a companion. As a little girl she used to dream of marrying her prince, but as she grew older the thought rarely seemed to surface to the front of her mind. She considered the idea now with a new excitement. She agreed to meet Martin, which was much to his delight as it was to hers.

Martin had spent all week worrying about his first meeting with Fiona. Indeed, he kept reminding himself that it was his *first* meeting; he had hoped that there would be many others after it. He knew he couldn't mess it up. He needed to do something special to show his interest in this lady. He had decided that he would present Fiona with a picnic, and prayed that she would not find this option for spending their afternoon too dull.

He didn't have a lot of money, and preparations for the occasion had cost him most of his wages, but something told him in the bottom of his heart that it would all be worth it. He had rummaged around in the back of the closet until he found his mother's old tartan picnic blanket, before bundling the red cloth into a large wicker basket. He took a strip of ribbon decorated with little red and white checks out of an old sewing basket and tied it to one of the handles of the basket. It would add a nice touch to the appearance of the basket, he thought, hoping Fiona would appreciate it.

Martin put just as much thought into the contents of the basket as he did its exterior. He filled it with an assortment of treats that he planned to share with Fiona. He cut a few thick slices of bread from a fresh white loaf, and wedged in between them a layer of mild cheddar cheese as a satisfying sandwich filling. He bought two triangles of a soft sponge cake, one for each of them, complete with layers of sticky strawberry jam and sweet vanilla butter icing. After cooking two sausages and allowing them to cool down, he chopped them up into little bite-size pieces. He had bought them from Fletcher's, the local butcher's down the street, and when Martin had explained in excitement to Mr Fletcher that he was taking a young lady out for what he hoped would be a romantic picnic, Mr Fletcher had kindly provided the meat at a discount price.

As an extra special treat, Martin had spent all morning attempting to bake a small batch of dry sugar biscuits to take with them. He'd thought about just going to the baker's to buy one for himself and one for Fiona, but he decided that he wanted to scrape together the last of his money to buy the ingredients to bake them himself, considering it to be a more personal gesture. It hadn't occurred to him during preparing the ingredients that he had never baked before. His mother was never known for her cooking abilities either; in fact, Martin couldn't remember ever seeing his mother baking anything. Nevertheless he was prepared to give it a go, and hoped for the best in the process. He was quite pleased with the outcome. The edges of the biscuits were only a little burned, and they were only slightly more squint than they were circular. He was sure that they were going to taste better than they looked.

Martin gathered everything together and laid them out on the kitchen table. He bundled each article inside a little paper napkin and placed them carefully inside the wicker basket. He had considered hanging the basket onto the handles of his bicycle, but when he looked at the patches of rust that had begun to form on its frame, he decided that the gesture would probably not be as romantic as he would have hoped. Instead, he took the short walk through the woods, swinging the basket merrily from his arm as he went, and headed straight for Fiona's house.

She greeted him at the door with a smile spread across her face. Martin couldn't help but notice straight away that her eyes sparkled as the light of the sunshine bounced from them. It was the same twinkle that caused him to fall in love with her that very evening as they lay beneath the silver light of the moon.

Fiona had thought it would be best if they didn't stray too far away from her house. She wanted to be nearby in case her father needed her for anything. Of course, William wasn't going to disturb his daughter while she was getting to know the boy he had hoped she'd marry. He wanted the evening to go as well for them both as they did, and so he had tried to persuade Fiona that he was very happy for her to take a walk down to the seaside if they wished. Fiona had refused though, insisting that she stayed near to the house.

"I'm sure this spot will be just perfect," Fiona exclaimed. Martin proceeded to spread out the picnic blanket on the grassy bank. They had walked a little further downstream than they had first intended to, but they'd managed to find a shaded patch of grass beneath some trees by the riverside. Fiona sat herself down on the blanket and stretched out her legs.

"It's very peaceful here, isn't it?" she spoke, resting on the back of her arms as Martin sat himself down beside her. "I could sit and watch the river all day. It flows so beautifully and gentle, don't you agree? But did you know that that's only on the surface? Underneath, where all the sharp rocks lie, the water is very fierce. Father has always warned me not to go too near the edge in case I was to fall in." She cast her eyes over the River Don, its waters gently lapping against the edges of the bank.

"I suppose looks can often be deceiving." Martin stretched over from where he sat and reached for a stone that lay on the grass. Having hurled it through the air, it landed in the river, splashing the water out into little ripples.

Fiona turned to look at Martin. Martin's eyes locked directly with hers. He couldn't help but notice how beautifully they resembled the excitement of the water as it swished rapidly down its course. Her eyes seemed to flicker with energy, and yet at the same time they remaining so tranquil, full of peace. Fiona gazed into Martin's own eyes as she spoke. "Do you read poetry, Martin?"

"I'm afraid that I don't." Martin was worried that that was not the answer she was looking for.

"Oh, is that so?"

He wondered if he should tell her the truth. "It's not that I wouldn't like to read poetry. I'm sure that I would find it very enjoyable. So often have I heard others speak of how they have been moved by such marvelous words. It's just that I'm not very good at reading." His cheeks turned a light red as he blushed through his embarrassment.

Martin's confession had not been entirely truthful. More accurately was the case that Martin couldn't read at all. Beyond the basic level of schooling where he had learned to spell his own name and make out the vowels of the alphabet, he had never learned the ability to understand how to read. He had tried to teach himself as the years went on, and had frequently asked his mother to find him a tutor, but she repeatedly told him that there was no way that they could afford one. He wasn't sure how truthful his mother was being, especially as he would watch her splashing on perfumes from fancy bottles, or dabbing posh rouge into her cheeks, but Martin continued to try with all of his energy to learn to read. As he grew older though he began to lose faith, and eventually stopped trying all together.

"Perhaps I could teach you one day," Fiona suggested. "There's this wonderful poem by this English poet called William Wordsworth. He was one of the greatest writers of all time, I think, and he wrote this poem called 'The River Derwent'. That's a river in England somewhere. In this poem he talks about the way river murmurs. Don't you think that's such a beautiful image?" Martin didn't answer her, but smiled as he continued to stare deep into Fiona's eyes. "He relates the river to his childhood and kind of compares it to humankind. He has such a wonderful ability to paint these vivid pictures with such powerful imagery."

Martin had never experienced so much passion in another human being before. His evening with Fiona had completely blown him away. The words she spoke, the love in her heart, and the light in her eyes; everything, down to the little uneven curl of dark hair that seemed to spiral down the left side of her face, ignited in him new emotions that he never knew he could feel. He fell in love with each and every aspect of her. Less than a week later, he had asked her to be his wife.

Fiona swallowed down the last of her supper as she turned to Martin, the conversation still on Martin's day. "Doesn't he have a wife and children at home?"

"I believe he has two boys. Thomas and....and...oh, now what did he say the wee baby was called again?" He picked at his tooth with a dirty finger as he tried to dislodge a piece of crust.

"I don't know if you ever mentioned the name to me. I just remember you saying that he had been born earlier than expected, the poor lamb." Fiona replied, before turning around to put the plates from supper into the bowl that sat on the counter. She brushed the crumbs away from the table into her hand, and, upon opening the kitchen window slightly, tossed them out onto the grass outside for the birds.

"I really can't remember. That's going to annoy me now. I'll have to ask him in the morning."

"That's if he's still there."

"I'm sure he'll be fine. I know he can be a bit clumsy some of the time, but he does seem to be quite a hard worker, and I'm sure the master will be able to see that."

Fiona turned her attention to the bowl of water and plunged the plates into it. She swirled the water around with her hands as she let it wash over the plates. She tried to ignore how cold the water had turned since she had heated it up that morning, running a ragged sponge over them to wipe away the smears of butter. "I hope you're right. I can't imagine how they would be able to cope if he was out of a job. We find it hard enough to get by with just the two of us." She drained the bowl out of the window as the dirty water splashed down onto the grass outside.

"We do manage to get by okay though, don't we?" Martin turned around in his chair to look at his wife, who had proceeded to dry the plates with a scruffy looking cloth.

"I've never really placed any great deal of importance on financial wealth." The tone in her voice was almost vacant as she avoided the question directly. "We never had a lot of money when I was growing up, so I've never really felt a desire for it. Father and I always seemed to be quite happy."

"And we are happy, aren't we?"

"Of course, Martin. We are happy."

"I'm glad!" He pushed out his chair and stood up. "Thank you for the supper. I must be off to bed now. It's been a long day, and I fear tomorrow will be even longer!" he said before kissing Fiona on the cheek. "Goodnight." With that, he left the room.

Fiona continued to stare out of the window. She could see the moon glowing above her, as the stars danced and twinkled in the darkness. For some reason, though, she couldn't find it within her to enjoy the beauty of the night sky like she usually could. She focused on the emptiness of the air outside, the cold breeze whipping in through the window and filling the kitchen with a soothing chill. Her eyes were silent, her heart motionless. Finally, she whispered, "goodnight."

After a restless sleep, Martin finally gave in and clambered out of bed. He made for the kitchen as he padded across the floor with bare feet, the worn roughness of the old carpet itchy and irritating him as he walked. On the side of the kitchen counter Fiona had left him a glass of water. She had done this every night for as long as he could remember. Martin regularly woke up thirsty, and it was the least she could do for her husband before she went to bed so that it saved him the trouble of having to enter the threatening night air to bring in the water.

He gulped down the drink and allowed the cold liquid to quench his dehydration. He knew he should have had something to drink before he went to bed; the bread had been delicious, but he should have known that it would cause his mouth to go dry in the middle of the night. He spluttered slightly as he took another sip, accidentally spraying some of the water onto the counter.

Martin drained the glass. He swished the towel rag that Fiona had left folded on the side of the bench around it to give it a quick clean, before returning the glass to the cupboard. He was just about to leave the room, when he decided that it would probably be best if he mopped up the water that he had spluttered. He dabbed at the surface of the counter in the dark with the rag, hoping that he was absorbing all of the right places. It was then that his right hand knocked against something hard.

"I wonder what she's been reading," Martin wondered to himself, as he recognised the object as being a book. Since he had long escaped the state of wanting to sleep, he pulled out a candle and set it down on the table. Lighting it, the room became cast in a warm glow. He took the book from the side of the counter where Fiona had left it, and sat down at the table with his back to the window.

Martin studied the cover of the book carefully. He ran his fingers over the lettering that was displayed on the front. He didn't know why he always did that. He supposed it was a habit he hadn't lost after he had developed it when Fiona began to teach him how to read. He said that it helped to give him a feel for the words if he touched them with the tip of his fingers. Fiona had been successful in teaching her husband, but it still often took him some time to finish reading full sentences due to the decline in his self-confidence over the years. Having seen Fiona read this particular book many times before though, Martin instantly recognised the name of the writer on the cover. "Lord Byron," he spoke out loud to himself as he acknowledged the poet.

Fiona would often talk about Lord Byron's poetry when she discussed her love of nature with Martin, but it was for one of Byron's poems in particular towards which Fiona had expressed a great deal of love. Martin adored hearing her recite it to him, so much so that he decided that he was going to memorise it himself so that he could say it to her on the day of their wedding. As he was concluding the last line of the poem, trying to hold back the croak in his throat that he knew was going to turn into a sob, he whispered the poem softly to his new bride. She burst into an uncontrollable river of tears. There hadn't been many people present to see them tie the knot, but Fiona's father, who had been feeling incredibly weak and near the end of his journey, had cried more on that day than Fiona had ever seen him do in her entire life.

Martin turned to where Fiona had left something inside the book. He had expected it to just be one of the bookmarks Fiona had fashioned - she occasionally liked to fold over an old note and doodle little hearts and patterns of stars onto it - but instead he found an unexpected sheet of paper. Fiona had folded it over in half, but there were no patterns or decorations on it. Curious, Martin opened it up with the assumption that he would find a note of some kind. What he found instead was four lines.

> *To melt black ice of forbidden love*
> *And spread the wings of an unsung song*
> *Is to cast dark thoughts to the sky above*
> *And exist in a world of sinful wrong.*

He stared for a moment, studying the shapes of the words. He took his time as he made out the first line, wondering why Fiona was writing about winter. She had never been very fond of the colder weather, much preferring the brightly coloured flowers and warm sunshine. He continued his way down the lines, casting his eyes back and forth as he tried to understand the words in front of him.

Suddenly, it hit him. He hoped in his heart that his lack of experience with poetry meant that he had completely misinterpreted his wife's words, for all he really knew about poetry was what Fiona had taught him. He was sure that he still had a lot to learn, and that he hadn't read the lines properly, but the lonely tear that rolled its way down his cheek told him that he believed otherwise. He let her words spin around in his head for a second, drowning his mind in a whirl of negative thoughts.

He stared blankly into the flame of the candle as

it flickered in the draft of the room. The unexpected hurt he had been hit with disappeared in his eyes, quickly to be replaced with a surge of anger. Crumpling the piece of paper up into his balled fist, he growled to himself. "She's in love with somebody else."

Chapter Eleven

Deep inside of me I can feel an ache. It's a pain that I am sure I've felt before, and yet somehow it feels strange, alien. It is the agony of a soul whose world has been ripped away from his very core. The threads of his existence have been tangled. I feel myself becoming overwhelmed with an unexpected sense of loss, a grieving for something that once existed, but is now withered, broken.

I open my eyes. I have ended up on my hands and knees, the coarse ground beneath me once again more real than life itself. I look up and see that Angel Ariana is opposite me still. She illuminates the space around her, the gentle waves of her golden hair allowing the soft glow to highlight her features in a loving warmth.

The silver river of light that was previously

between us is no longer there, but I can sense that we are still somehow connected. Her wings seem even larger than before; the feathers appear more plump and wide, each one having spread itself out. They're all curved down towards the floor, guiding the gentle curves of the wings.

I begin to weep. As I am overcome with the sadness of another, I struggle to control my emotions. They are no longer my own. The ache in my back moves its way down my spine. The marks on my cheek start to itch once more. They are real, they exist. They are my own. I can look past this physical pain though. Inside I feel only the heartache that has been born out of the vision shown to me by my guardian angel. My heart is shattered. Torn. Alone.

Angel Ariana speaks to me; her voice is melodic as it relieves the strain on my heart. She tells me not to worry. She says that I have nothing to fear. I know she is right. I inhale deeply as I try to slow down my breathing. Amidst the thick dirt of the air I can taste the purity and the holiness of my angel's presence. It's a power like nothing else I've ever experienced.

She tells me that I need to stand up, that I am to regain control of my own emotions. I listen to Angel Ariana's words and use all of my strength to force my tired body up. I rest for a moment on my knees before managing to use the wall to lift myself the rest of the way. I feel drained, void of all my own strength, but it is being engulfed in the love of my guardian angel that provides me with the ability to keep going.

I no longer feel alone. I no longer feel afraid. She tells me to listen. As I do so, I can hear it floating through the air again. The sweet music, a tune so faint and distant yet somehow coming right from my very core. From the heart of my guardian angel. I think I recognise it, but I cannot be sure. It calms me, soothing away all distress and negativity. I close my eyes to listen more closely.

There is a gentle echo to the music. The way the notes of the violin blend in harmony with the delicate sounds of the organ floods my heart with warmth. I can hear a flute sounding distantly. It's beautiful, inviting. As I focus on the music, I imagine myself standing proud on the top of a large green hill; the wind is wild as it whips around me; I look out to sea and watch from the great height as the water becomes the center of my attention. It makes me feel free and alive.

I open my eyes as the music begins to fade. Angel Ariana does not speak now, but I can see that there is a certain look in her eyes that has changed. Her dress no longer flows in the gentle breeze, but remains still and silent. Her eyes are flooded with compassion; it's almost a sympathy that I cannot know about. As she looks down into my own eyes I can feel her looking right through into my own soul. The light around my guardian angel begins to fade, the bright golden glow slowly transforming until it dims down into little more than a slight tint. Angel Ariana smiles at me. I know that I am not to worry.

I watch in amazement as she starts to become translucent. Through the light of her dress I can see the solid wall behind her, lit up slightly to reveal the solid lumps of dirt, the shards of stones, the clumps of soil that have emerged between the suffocating brickwork.

I start to panic as I watch her fade. I want to cry

out to her. Please stay with me, Angel Ariana. Don't leave me alone. I quiver at the thought of being on my own again. But my eyes remain without tears, my throat dry. She is almost gone now, a faint shadow of a light in front of me. She does not answer my cries. Instead, she whispers something to me before she fades away completely.

She is gone. I slam my hands firm against the wall behind where she previously stood, before allowing my body to slump against it. In the darkness I can see nothing. I am all alone again. All of the pain I felt before, all my own emotions, all my own agonies have returned. My heart begins to beat faster. I try not to panic as I slide my back down the wall and crumple onto the floor. I feel confused, scared. I turn Angel Ariana's words around in my head as I struggle to work out what she means.

You must grow.

Chapter Twelve

They had been informed that there was nothing that they could do. They had tried everything, they assured the couple, but they were afraid that it was too late. They assured them that it wasn't anybody's fault. Nobody should blame themselves for what had happened. It was one of those unfortunate things in life that could not be foreseen; it could not have been prevented.

Peter had been at work all day. A delivery of orders for the office had not long arrived: paper clips, manila folders, that sort of thing. He was busying himself with popping a large sheet of bubble wrap when he heard the phone ring. He considered ignoring it. He could let the call go straight to voicemail. They could leave a message if it was important. He'd get to it when he wasn't busy. He glanced at the screen out of curiosity to see who was bothering him. When he noticed Maggie's number flash up on the screen, however, something inside of him made pick up the phone. Maggie never phoned him when he was at work. Slightly anxious, Peter pressed the little green phone icon to activate the call.

"Margaret. What is it? You know I'm at work." He tried to mask any hint of concern that was in his voice from his wife.

Peter could hear a crying on the other end of the phone. It took a few seconds for Maggie to be able to compose herself before she could manage to speak. "Peter, you need to come home. It's Thomas..." Peter didn't wait for Maggie to finish speaking as she burst into tears down the phone. He told her that he would leave immediately, and hung up the phone.

He flew down the three flights of stairs from his office and raced across the car park. He didn't slow down as he continued to speed his way back home. His heart was racing. Thoughts were running through his head as he was forced to wait at the traffic lights. Had he fallen? Had he bumped his head? Was his arm broken? He needed to get to him, and fast.

The ambulance was already parked outside of his front door when Peter pulled the car up outside the flat. He jumped out, and slammed the door shut on the bottom of his jacket as he hurried. He didn't notice that it was stuck as he dived down the path towards the building, ripping the side of his jacket as it tore away from the car door. He wouldn't have cared; he had to get to the boy.

Peter flung the front door open and halted as he took in what was in front of him. At the end of the hall, in the doorway to the living room, he could see that Maggie had collapsed onto her hands and knees on the floor. She couldn't stop crying. She was wailing almost. Near her Peter saw two paramedics; one stood in front of her with his hands slouched in his pockets, while the other crouched down by Maggie's side trying to support her. Deep down she appreciated their attempts to comfort her, but she knew it wasn't going to make any difference.

Peter pulled his mind to a focus as he raced down the corridor. He hadn't bothered to stop and shut the front door behind him. The paramedic who had been standing in front of Maggie noticed this as Peter entered the room, and walked down the hall to shut it on Peter's behalf. It was the least he could do.

"Margaret? Margaret!" Peter couldn't hide his panic any longer. He cast his eyes all around the living room, almost spinning in a circle as he looked for the child. "Where is he, Margaret? Where's Thomas?!"

Maggie was unable to reply. One of the paramedics was trying to calm her down, telling her that she had to take deep breaths. She listened to his words and attempted to slow her breathing down as instructed, but still she cried uncontrollably.

The other paramedic, who was wearing a plastic tag on his pocket to indicated that his name was Bill, turned to Peter and gestured for him to sit down on the sofa. Peter did as he was asked, struggling to think clearly. Bill took it upon himself to sit to the other side of Peter.

"What is it? What's happened? Where's my son?" His words were frantic.

"He's in the ambulance just now with a few of my colleagues. We really are very sorry. We did everything we possibly could." Bill could tell by the look on Peter's face that Maggie hadn't been able to tell him why she had phoned for the ambulance for Thomas. As he explained to Peter what had happened to his son, Peter's heart sank deep into his chest.

Maggie had never seen Peter cry before. Sure, she'd seem him well up a few times, but it was rare that he would show any sort of strong emotions in front of his wife. He never cried in front of anybody, for that matter. But when the sudden realisation sunk in about the reality of little Thomas, Peter had sobbed. He could feel his heart coming up through his chest and into his throat. His own son, his little Thomas. His precious baby. How could this have happened? He couldn't understand it.

The other paramedic in the flat, who had introduced himself as Andy, had explained to Maggie and Peter that Sudden Infant Death Syndrome is one of those horrible things in life that couldn't possibly have been foreseen.

"Cot death," Peter whispered a response.

"It's usually very unexpected, and I'm afraid that we are rarely able to find any cause for the death. Unfortunately, this appears to be the case with your son, Mr Gordon." Andy spoke sensitively as he explained the situation to Thomas's parents

Peter was unable to speak. His throat had dried up. His mind was blank. All he was able to see was Thomas's beautiful little face. He was smiling up at him with his toothless gums. His dainty button nose, the rosy red apples of his cheeks; his watery eyes gazing up at him, so wide and full of carefree curiosity.

Andy carried on talking to Peter as he tried to explain what steps would have to be taken next, but

Peter was no longer listening. Instead, he had closed his eyes and was concentrating on the image of his little boy that he refused to let slip out of his mind.

Thomas was always such a happy, healthy baby. He had been born close to his due date, arriving into the world only a few days before he was expected. Peter remembered the way Thomas had grabbed hold of his father's finger with a delicate hand when he was only three days old. Peter was faced with more love than he had ever experienced in his entire life, as it spiraled right through him to take over his every fiber of existence.

Peter hadn't planned to take any time off work when Thomas was born. He decided Maggie would be able to cope just fine on her own when Thomas came along; after all, it was a woman's duty to take care of the children. But as soon as he looked down into his son's face when the nurse placed him in his arms, Peter knew there and then that he would have to be with his child. He couldn't help but fall instantly in love with this tiny human being. He wanted to spend every second that he could with him. He couldn't believe it. He had been given a *son*.

He knew that he would have to teach Thomas to play football the moment that he was able to walk and run around. When Peter was a child, his own father, Mac Gordon, used to take him to Duthie Park every Sunday morning, allowing his mother to stay at home so she could cook the roast dinner. They would have a kick around with a ball for a good hour or so. Mac would always be the one in goal. They'd place their jumpers in two bundles with a few meters in between them, and Mac would stand in the middle, pretending that he was concentrating really hard on the ball when it came rolling towards him. Right at the last second, when Peter thought the ball was about to be stopped by the goalkeeper, Mac would clumsily swing his leg in the wrong direction, or kick with his wrong foot, always intentionally allowing the ball to slip through into the makeshift goal.

If it was a sunny day, Mac would take Peter to the ice cream van that used to stop next to the pool at the entrance of the park. He would buy them both a cone, always allowing Peter to have a flake in his ice cream, and sometimes he'd even be allowed chocolate sprinkles too if Mac was feeling extra generous that day. "Don't tell your mother though!" He used to warn Peter, with a grin spread across his face as they would sit on the park bench and lick at their treats beneath the warmth of the sun. "She'd only have a go at me for ruining your appetite before dinner!"

To warm them back up after they'd indulged in their delicious ice creams, Mac and Peter used to take a walk through the greenhouses that were situated at the top of the park. Mac had been a keen gardener in his day and used to keep an allotment so he could grow his own vegetables, so they always found this trip quite fascinating. One summer Mac decided that he wanted to grow strawberries. He let Peter help with picking them when they were ready, before they mashed some in a bowl and sprinkled them with sugar for dessert. Peter used to love listening to his father's talks as they would walk round; Mac would often point at a plant and instantly name it for his son, before telling Peter all about how it grew and if it needed any special foods to keep it strong. Of course, Mac could have been talking about anything in the world. It wouldn't have mattered to Peter. He always cherished the times he spent alone with his father at the weekends.

When he was nine years old, Peter's weekend trips to the Duthie Park with Mac came to an end. There was no more football. There was no more ice cream.

There had been a fight. It must have been on a Sunday, because Peter had remembered that the gravy boat had ended up on the floor, upside down. He had been in the middle of chewing a slice of carrot when he was ordered to leave the room. To this day, Peter still couldn't eat carrots without being transported back to the day that ruined his life.

He hid under his duvet on his bed to block out the shouting. Even with his pillow pressed firmly over his ears, though, Peter was still able to hear the row that carried its way throughout the house. What were they saying? Their voices were too muffled to tell.

He decided to be brave and creep across his bedroom to the top of the landing, his youthful curiosity getting the better of him. He stood for a moment, just out of sight in case anybody came up, and listened. His father was angry, he could tell that. His voice was raised. Peter had only ever heard Mac shout once before, and that was when he had accidentally slammed the cupboard door on his finger. He swore a lot then.

He was swearing now too. Lots and lots of bad words that made Peter gasp. He heard something smash – a plate, perhaps – and ran back into his bedroom. He began to shake in fear, terrified of the chaos. What was going on? Why were they shouting? He curled back up under his duvet and hugged his teddy bear tightly. He cried into Max's soft fur, turning the beige of his fluffy coat into a damp dark brown with his salty tears. He prayed that the noise would stop soon.

Peter had fallen asleep, his face still pressed against Max, but he was startled awake when he heard feet thundering up the stairs. In the room next door he heard somebody violently tear back the zip of a bag. He listened to the clattering of clothes hangers that followed.

He peered out of the bed covers to see what was going on. Upon pulling the duvet back, he slid out of bed and walked across to his bedroom door. It was only open ajar so he couldn't see anything. He listened for a moment before opening it fully. "Dad?"

"Peter," came his father's reply. He was busy folding his shirts into a large black holdall. Peter watched as he stuffed his ties hastily into the side pocket of the bag.

"Where are you going?" Peter swallowed back his tears. He didn't want his father to see that he was frightened.

Mac pulled open the top drawer of the wooden chest and rummaged around. When he found what he was looking for, he fished out a little tin box. From there he produced a rusty pocket watch. "This was your Grandfather's," he explained to Peter as he held it up.

"Granddad Joe?" Peter asked.

"The very man!" Mac placed the pocket watch on the side of the bed, and continued to pack his clothes into the holdall. Peter watched as he zipped the top of the bag up before heaving it onto his shoulder. He remembered to pick up the pocket watch. "Come on, Peter." He steered his son back into his own bedroom. "Sit down for a minute."

Peter sat on the bed on the spot where his father had patted. Mac knelt on the floor in front of him, the holdall resting to the side.

"Peter, I've got to go away for a bit. I don't know when I'll be back, but I need you to behave for your mother. I'm sure she'll take good care of you while I'm gone." Mac could feel himself starting to well up. Peter noticed the crackle in his father's voice.

"But I don't want you to go!" he protested.

"I know, son. I know. But you have to understand that this is something I have to do. I promise it won't be for too long. While I'm away though, I want you to look after this for me." He handed Peter the pocket watch. "It's very old, remember, so you need to take extra special care of it. Do you think you can do that for me?"

Peter studied the object that had been given to him. "Yes," he sniffed in reply.

"Good. Now, come here and give me a hug." Mac leaned forward so that Peter could wrap his arms around his neck. He started sobbing into his father's ear. A single tear made its way down Mac's own cheek. He managed to wipe it away before Peter noticed. Standing up again, he grabbed the holdall and started for the door. "Goodbye, Peter."

"I love you, Dad." Peter squeaked between tears, unable to control the quiver in his voice.

Mac looked at Peter for a moment. "I love you too, son." He left the room, closing the door behind him.

To this day he didn't know how Mac had found out, but Peter's mother Dorothy had been having an affair. For how long, he didn't know, but it didn't matter to Mac. As soon as he discovered that his wife had so much as touched another man, he knew he couldn't be with her any more. Mac went to live with his sister Polly for a while. He wrote a letter to Peter when he arrived there, and told him all about how, someday, once Mac had found his feet, Peter could come and visit him and his Aunt Polly in Stonehaven. He explained that they would be able to make sandcastles on the beach together, and chase the waves before running away from them as they followed them back up the sand. They could go for picnics too, Mac explained, and have salmon sandwiches and ready salted crisps and chocolate cake. Aunt Polly would make some of her delicious fresh orange juice, and they could go for long bike rides in the afternoons. Just the two of them.

But Peter never did get to run along the sands of Stonehaven. He never tasted Aunt Polly's fresh orange juice, and he didn't go for any bike rides. Eventually, his father started to write to him less and less. He would send a birthday card every year, but on the day of his thirteenth birthday Peter waited patiently by the door for his father's annual note, only to find that the postman didn't deliver anything.

He never heard from his father again. In later years, he learned that Mac had gone on to marry somebody else, a blonde woman whose name Peter had chosen to not remember. His Aunt Polly had written to Peter some years later when he was in his early twenties to explain that Mac had passed away suddenly. "It was a heart attack," she announced. The news had shocked Peter into great sadness.

Peter resented his mother his whole life. She had been the reason his father went away. She had been the reason he had to grow up without a Dad. She didn't even have the decency to marry the person she'd been having an affair with. Peter was disgusted, ashamed of her. She'd deprived him of his own father, and he was sure she didn't even care. She was an embarrassment to him.

Peter had returned to the Winter Gardens in the Duthie Park a few times over the years, and always made a point of paying a visit to it every year on the anniversary of his father's death. The moment he would walk into the hot glass house, he would become instantly overwhelmed by the luscious scent of all the tropical plants mixing together in harmony as it hit him full force.

As he made his way through the opening he would stop to throw a penny in the direction of the mechanical frog as it moved up and down in its little pond of water. Continuing through to the back of the Gardens, he would pause to say hello to the golden fish as they shimmered beneath the mini bridge.

Peter would find a vacant bench, and there he would sit on his own, in the silence of his own thoughts, often losing track of time. Around him he could see only the bright colours of the flowers as they burst out of the rich greenery of the trees and the tropical plants. He would become enveloped by the aroma of the room, allowing himself to feel, if just for a moment, at one with nature. He was at peace with the world when he visited there.

He would always remember to take the pocket watch along with him. It was still ticking away after all those years. As he sat, he turned it around in his hand several times before holding it tightly in his palm and saying a prayer for Mac. Peter may not have had any strong beliefs about the afterlife, but he did believe in his father.

When Thomas was born, Peter vowed that he would spend every second that he was able to with his son. He wasn't going to let anybody get in the way of their relationship together. He couldn't wait to buy him his first football and take him to the same park that he used to go to with his own father. They would eat ice creams together in the same spot by the entrance. Together they would create happy memories just like the ones Peter had enjoyed as a boy. Thomas had been only five months old when Peter's plans were forced to come to an abrupt end.

A pattern of white frills made its way around the card to create a border, which Maggie had fashioned out of an old doily. Across the top of the scrapbook feature there was a little foam stalk carrying a light blue bundle in its beak as it flew. Beneath it Maggie had painted white fluffy clouds, shading them slightly with a soft shade of blue to match the colour of the background of the display.

Across the bottom of the page in a cream coloured banner she had written her son's name. *Thomas Michael Gordon* was displayed proudly in swirly silver lettering. Underneath it Maggie had written a date: 5.5.1997. Thomas's birthday.

Peter couldn't take his eyes away from the photo as it stared at him from the center. It had been taken on the day that he had arrived, just hours after his birth. His tiny fists were clenched, and he was waving them in the air above his head. He was sound asleep. Maggie had dressed him in a brand new white baby grow, which turned out to be a size or two too large for him. On his head rested a soft cotton hat. He was a vision of innocence.

His eyes were squinted shut in the photo. Peter didn't need them to be open though; he could still see them, each one a watery pool of blue. His little boy's pupils were piercing, full of life and happiness. He had Peter's eyes, and his nose too. Peter knew he would have grown up to be a very handsome man.

To stop him from welling up as he looked at the photo, Peter lifted his glass and emptied it. Swallowing, he felt the comfort of the burning liquid as it ran down his throat and made its way to his core.

Maggie was still huddled on the floor in front of the radiator, her arms remaining wrapped tightly around her as she sobbed into her knees. She had curled her feet towards her, trying to protect herself from the outside world that demanded her attention.

"It was your fault," Peter said, almost under his breath.

Maggie didn't respond. Peter filled his glass again from the bottle of vodka that sat next to the scrapbook, and gulped down a mouthful before returning it to the table.

"Did you hear me, Margaret?" He walked towards her. "I said it was all *your* fault!" He nudged her ankle with his boot. His anger began to increase again when she didn't react. He wasn't going to allow his wife to ignore him. He swung his leg backwards and proceeded to boot her full force in the shin, making sure he hit the bruise from the previous impact. The strike forced Maggie to draw her entire body further inwards as she moved closer into to the wall behind her.

Before Maggie had a chance to cry out in pain, Peter had clenched his right hand around the top of her left arm and was hauling her up. He flung her onto her feet, before pushing her across to the other side of the room. Maggie could just about find the strength to summon stability to prevent her from falling down onto her hands and knees. She couldn't stop herself from stumbling into the side of the table though. She clutched onto her side in pain as the corner of the furniture collided with her body just below the rib cage.

Peter walked slowly towards her, taking his time with each step. His eyes were open wide and flooded with malice. Sweat had begun to emerge on his forehead. His veins were flowing with rage, his fists clenched thick by his side as he staggered towards her.

"You, my sweet," he stood in front of Maggie now, "were a terrible mother. Did you know that?" He wasn't touching her, but there was barely an inch of space between them. Maggie placed her hands on the edge of the table to support her exhausted body and leaned back as far as she could. She had no choice but to turn her head to the right to escape the stench of Peter's alcoholic breath, even if it did mean she was leaving her face exposed and vulnerable to his hands. She tried to focus on the sound of the rain as it lashed against the window. Anything to try and take her mind away from what was happening.

"Well?" He whispered close to her ear, leaning in. "Did you?!" He shouted this time, his voice booming into Maggie's head. She jumped, at which point Peter slammed his hand down onto the top of her shoulder so that she was unable to move anywhere. He couldn't let his dear sweet Maggie run away from him, now, could he?

"It was all your fault, Margaret. Entirely your doing. *You* took the only good thing in my life away from me. *You* killed my son, Margaret. *You* killed my Thomas."

Thomas. Her precious little boy. Maggie turned and noticed the scrapbook that lay open by her right side. She looked fondly at her little cherub shining brightly in the photo. There wasn't a day that went by when she didn't think about him. He was such a good little boy, such a happy, playful child. Even at such a young age he always seemed to be so aware of his surroundings.

"You're scum, Margaret. Filthy, dirty, worthless scum." Peter began viciously prodding all over his wife's body with his index fingers. Her arms. Her thighs. Her stomach. Maggie winced as he repeatedly poked at her, but she knew that the real pain was in her heart. Her own tears began to cascade as she ached for her little boy.

Peter grabbed hold of her face and squeezed her cheeks with his hand as he held her tightly. He forced her head to turn round so that she had no choice but to look right at him. "Look at the state of you." He lifted his thumbs up towards her face. He pressed them against Maggie's eyelids, smearing her dark make up.

He moved his right hand so that it was firmly clamped on the back of her neck, tugging beneath her hair. She could feel his clasp becoming tighter.

He firmed his grip as he moved it round her face, cupping the side of her jaw as he stared deep into her eyes. He didn't say anything, but glared as if trying to bury his way down into her soul. Maggie was sure her heart had already been ripped out of her chest; there surely couldn't be much left for Peter to destroy.

"You need a haircut," he finally spoke as he flicked at a strand of her hair. It now hung all around her shoulders. The time she spent trying to make it look presentable for Lucy's birthday meal might not have existed now. "Blonde hair makes your face look really disgusting. It's so cheap and dirty. You're an embarrassment," he spat. He began twisting the strand around his finger as he spoke, releasing it before twisting it again, only tighter. Maggie didn't expect Peter to like her hair; she could cope with his insults. She mustn't allow his words to affect her.

"I want you to get rid of it."

Maggie snapped her full attention back to Peter in shock. He would complain about her hair often, but she knew by the bitterness in his voice that this was a genuine order. She didn't know what to think. She didn't know what to say.

"I...I will," she managed to respond. "On Monday. I'll go to the hairdressers. I'll ask them to..." She was whimpering, trying to take care of her words so as to not induce any more anger in Peter. She needed to entertain his ideas to keep him happy. She was sure he would forget the conversation in the morning.

"No, Margaret. That's not good enough." His hot breath sprayed against her face as he stepped closer. "I want you to get rid of it *now*." As the last syllable of his command echoed around the room, Peter pushed Maggie back into the table before he stormed off into the kitchen. Maggie was too frightened to feel the strength of the pain as her spine crashed into the wooden edge; she knew she had to concentrate on Peter, unsure of what was happening.

She could hear him rummaging for something in one of the drawers, but she couldn't see him. She was unable to move from where she stood cowering against the table. She didn't know what was going on. She was frozen, terrified.

A few moments later Peter emerged back into the living room. Maggie gasped when she saw what he was gripping onto with his tight fist. As she inhaled she started coughing, but this ended abruptly when Peter slammed his free hand hard against her chest. "Shut up!" he ordered. He didn't want to be able to hear her while he concentrated.

He held up the scissors for Maggie to see. She tried to avoid looking at them as the light bounced off the shiny blades. "The thing is, Margaret, I hate people who make a fool of me. And when my wife doesn't make any effort to take care of the way she looks, I get *very, very* annoyed." He turned the scissors around in his hands. "Because when you look stupid, it makes me look stupid. Do you hear what I'm saying, Margaret?"

Maggie didn't know where to put her eyes. She was too scared to close them. Tears were streaming down her cheeks now. Peter had pressed his waist firm against her body so that her back was forced against the edge of the table. She couldn't move. She couldn't run. She couldn't hide.

"But we need to fix that, don't we? All it'll take is a little snip...snip...snip..." His words were slow. He opened and closed the scissors in harmony with each syllable as his eyes beamed at Maggie. She was sure she could hear the slicing of the blades as they collided together, echoing through her mind as a threat that she knew would never cease.

Peter lifted up a strand of Maggie's hair daintily in between his thumb and forefinger, and positioned the scissors with precision. "Are you ready?" He didn't wait for her to answer.

He closed the scissors down on Maggie's hair, cutting the strand directly below her ear. The hair parted and tumbled down to the ground, falling lifelessly. Continuing to work in the silence of the room, Peter took his time chopping the scissors through his wife's hair, taking care and precision over each move.

Maggie sobbed uncontrollably. She had forced herself to shut her eyes; she couldn't watch as Peter hacked away. He made sure he spent equal time on each snip. He was enjoying every second of it. The air around him grew thick with hatred.

Peter threw the scissors onto the floor. "Finished." Despite the absence of any emotion in his voice, his speech still seemed to sound sinister. "Well? Do you want to see it then or not?"

What was she supposed to say?

"Of course you do, Margaret. Don't move." Peter waltzed through to the bedroom and returned with the small mirror that was usually situated on top of the chest of drawers. He held it up in front of Maggie's face, but she kept her eyes tightly closed, with her face towards the ground.

"Come on, Margaret. Open your bloody eyes! Look at what I've done for you!" When Maggie was too frightened to obey his command, Peter lifted his hand and slapped his wife hard across the cheek. She bolted her head to the side as his palm smashed against her jaw. Peter grabbed hold of her neck as she moved, before thrusting the mirror in front of her. She was forced to face the damage.

Her beautiful hair. What had he done? Her own husband. Strands of blonde stuck out in tufts beneath her ears. He had attacked it right up to where her shortest layers had been at the back, so that it now sat permanently ruffled in a short, ragged, boyish bob. Maggie put her hands to her face as she tried to muffle her crying. Around her feet she could feel the dead hair as it tickled against her bare skin. Even after Peter had thrown the mirror behind him onto the sofa, Maggie couldn't escape the reality of what he had just done to her. She tried to step away, but Peter pushed her back.

"Don't even think about it. I'm not finished with you."

Chapter Thirteen

I struggle as I grow more isolated. I am aching, alone. I feel too weak to stand up by myself.

But at least I'm hidden away from the rest of the world. I know that I am safe here, secure within my walls. I should have nothing to fear but my own existence. But the noises, they infiltrate their way in from outside. They're fierce. With every bang that echoes its way in, with every screech that soars through the air, I cannot stop myself from flinching. I close my eyes as I try to block out my surroundings.

I wonder how long it's been since I last smiled. I may be safer in here, but it doesn't mean I'm happy. It is cold, dirty. Angel Ariana did cast the most beautiful light around me; I could use it to keep warm. But now that she has disappeared, I am once again faced with the silence that smothers the empty space.

I curl my knees up as I sit on the floor. My back is pressed firmly against the wall as I depend on its support. I can feel it solid behind me. There is nothing sturdier in the whole of my world, yet it continues to flake apart as I shift. I'm sure that it's going to crumble down any minute. The fragments of brickwork rub away as I wriggle to make myself more comfortable.

When I was a child I used to play in the comfort and safety of my shed. At the bottom of the garden we used to have a small wooden shed which nobody had any real use for. That was, until I decided to explore it one day. I don't really know where it came from, or why my parents even had a shed in the first place. It wasn't very big, but to my childhood curiosity it was a wonderful large home in which I could have many of my own private adventures.

I had begged and begged my parents to let me play in the shed. For what had felt like months to me they refused to give in to my request, telling me that it was too dangerous. It was certainly no place for a little girl to spend her time; I'd only ruin my pretty dresses. "I promise I'll only ever go in there when I have my garden clothes on, mummy!" I pleaded.

Eventually, after endless nagging and pestering, they gave in. My Dad set to work clearing out the small selection of objects that previously lived in there. Out came an old rusty toolbox, which was missing most of its red paintwork and all of its tools. There was a moss-green canvas of some sort, perhaps a part of a tent that we would never end up using. A few other bits and pieces were removed from the shed, but I'd asked if I could keep the flower pots in there just as they were about to be taken out with the rest of the items that were soon to be discarded. To my surprise, my Dad said yes.

I turned the large ceramic pot upside down so that I could use it as a seat. I would pretend that it was my very own throne. I was the Ruler of the Shed, and only I was allowed to be in there unless special orders by the Queen were given. I used the two other flower pots, which were much smaller in size compared to my throne, to store the essentials that I would need to keep in my shed. In one of the pots I decided to keep all of my coloured pencils from my crate in my bedroom; these were the ones I was allowed to take with me when I went outside. I always had to leave my special pencils behind, as they were just to be used for indoor projects where they wouldn't get dirty or damaged. In the second flower pot I kept a small stash of chocolates. I would take them back into the house with me every night so that they weren't nibbled at by bugs or insects, and then sneak them back out into my shed the next day. I didn't tell my Mum this though; I doubt she would have been pleased that her daughter was munching on chocolates that had been nesting inside an old flower pot.

I used to love taking my sketch pad down into my shed with me. I would close the door behind me and, using only the small stream of light that would trickle in from the tiny window that was situated on one of the shed's walls, I would sit myself down on my throne and sketch away for hours. Sometimes I would have to wrap up in extra thick layers, and when it was really cold – when the ground was littered with snowflakes, and frost had started to creep up the sides of my shed – I wasn't allowed to go in it at all. But if it was a sunny day I was allowed to spend as many hours as I wanted in there when I wasn't at school.

What I enjoyed most about being in my shed was the fact that I could be alone. I did like sitting in my room and drawing all afternoon with my fancy pencils, but there was something so much more magical about spending time in my shed. It allowed me to block out the outside world and concentrate only on what I wanted to.

Occasionally, a small creature would come by and visit me. I remember a little mouse popped by once whilst I was in the middle of sketching a lovely spring picture of a bunny rabbit hopping along in a meadow. I decided to name this mouse Marty. Once he had worked out how to get back out of the shed, however, which took him quite a bit of time as it didn't seem to occur to him that he could just creep back through the little hole in the corner from through which he had originally entered, I never saw him again. It had been nice to have his company for those few hours.

Right up until we moved house when I was ten years old, I pretty much lived in that shed. We weren't allowed to take it with us to the new place as we didn't have a very big garden, and suddenly I had been left with a large hole in my life. Without my shed, I had no way to relax. I had nowhere that I could escape to. I was being forced to exist in reality, and it was painful.

As I started to progress through the beginning of my teenage years, I found that I was spending more and more time locked away in my bedroom. I would frantically try and find a way to escape from my surroundings, but the search only made me more apprehensive about the material world around me. Everything seemed to irritate me. Everything was against me.

I tried to take long baths in the evening, soaking myself in so many bubbles that it had started to make my skin itch. I would constantly be listening to music to try and down out the chaotic noises that hurtled across the earth, plummeting into my mind at monumental speed. Listening to the radio all of the time allowed me to discover my love for classical and folk music, but it never seemed to provide me with a solution to my quest for a way out.

Then one day, everything changed when I decided that I would nip into the shop on the way home from school.

Ordinarily I would just rush straight home so that I could get on with completing any homework I had that evening, and then maybe work on my drawings for a bit. However, it was becomingly increasingly harder for me to concentrate on my artwork as the months went on. My images were becoming darker. The bunnies turned to skeletons; the meadows transformed into graveyards. I was becoming lost in a world over which I knew I had no control.

I was only going to go to the shop to pick up a bottle of water. We'd been playing volleyball in gym class in the afternoon and I'd not had a chance to quench my thirst since then. However, something happened to catch my eye as I walked by the magazine stand.

I had heard about spiritual energies before, but only vaguely. It wasn't something that I thought I would have come across in the local shop. I suppose I had always assumed that you'd only ever be able to learn about it from one of those dark and mysterious tents that always seem to be lurking at the back of carnivals. So when I noticed on the front of a glossy weekly magazine for women that there was an advert for an article inside that talked about meditation, I was instantly drawn to it.

I used the last of my pocket money to purchase the magazine, and hoped for the best. As soon as I arrived home less than half an hour later, I rushed up to my room and closed my bedroom door behind me. I decided it might be a good idea to keep the main light turned off, and just read by the soft light of my bedside lamp. I didn't know what to expect from this new discovery, but I decided to go into it with an open mind. I speed-read the article, which only took up half a page in the magazine, and reread it immediately after.

It seemed to be describing to me what sounded like the most sensational experience one could ever imagine. Was it possible that I could really become at one with my body and mind, and completely block out the world that surrounded me, yet still remain awake? This sounded exactly like what I was looking for.

The magazine article had suggested that I tried mediation with lit candles around me; apparently the soft glow of the flame would help to relax the mind. I remembered that I had a candle that I'd never used before in the bottom of my drawer. Having received it as a Christmas present from an Aunt the year previous, I had shoved it away out of sight, certain that I had no time for such things. I was thankful for the gift now though. In need of something to light it with, I bounded down the stairs and began raiding inside the kitchen cabinet for a box of matches.

I took the stairs two at a time back up to my bedroom, carrying the matches securely in my hand, before stopping for a moment outside my door as I caught my breath. I hopped onto my bed and sat cross-legged, almost bubbling over with excitement. This new energy was refreshing. It had been so long since I had been able to feel positive about something. I had begun to give up hope. After I made sure that the candle was standing upright on my bedside cabinet, I turned off the lamp so that I was now in complete darkness. All I had to do now was light the candle.

With caution, I struck the match and geared it towards the wick, having made sure the candle was not too close for me to accidentally knock it over during meditation. Steadying my hand, I lowered it down and set it still for a few seconds so that I could ensure that the wick was lit properly. Blowing out the match, I set it down on the bedside table and sat back.

The candle sat in a little glass stand, which somebody had tastefully decorated with little golden swirls to give it a more shiny, elegant appearance. The cream candle that stood upon the stand reflected its soft colour against the glass, creating a soft, soothing appearance.

The candlewick flooded the wall behind it with an image of its beautiful light. Its brightness illuminated its immediate surroundings, making its way over towards me. I watched as the little flame flickered in the natural breeze of the room.

I found myself staring at the candle for five

minutes, concentrating my attention on the dancing flame. I became transfixed by its beauty. I had been unable to avert my gaze for a few moments, mesmerised, before I remembered that the magazine had instructed that I had to close my eyes. I wasn't sure how this was going to work if I couldn't see the candle, but I had nothing to lose. I trusted the words of the article and closed my eyes.

As I rested my eye lids, I was sure that I could still see the golden glow of the candle that had started to take over the room. I inhaled, deeply filling my lungs with air. As I exhaled, I couldn't believe how quickly the tension I had felt all week in the back of my shoulders was beginning to diffuse. Was this meditation thing really working?

The air around me had started to fill with the delicious sweet vanilla scent of the candle as the wax began to melt. It was such a calming fragrance, as I absorbed it within me every time I breathed in. I continued to breathe slowly, and before long I found myself drifting off into my own mind.

I opened my eyes some time later. When I checked the clock on my wall, I noticed that nearly half an hour had passed by.

I couldn't believe it. I was sure I'd only been trying to meditate for two, maybe three minutes. It certainly hadn't felt as long as half an hour. The wax had started to form a pool around the wick of the candle, but the flame was still burning brightly. I had been completely alone with my mind, immersed in my own company.

I had finally found the cure to my own unhappiness from which I had spent so many years trying to escape.

From that point I became hooked on the idea of meditating. I visited the library in the city center later that week and checked out all of the books on meditating that I could find. I spent hours and hours after school pouring over them, discovering a whole world of new ideas and styles of meditation. There was so much that I had to learn; it was overwhelming, but exciting.

Though I did try out a few alternative methods suggested in some of the books from the library, I have always preferred to meditate with a candle glowing in front of me. The warmth of the scent helps soothe me. It quickly became a fundamental method in my own relaxation.

However, a few years ago I began to find myself in situations that would shake my breathing without warning. My mind would become flooded with negativity; my soul would be stabbed with hatred and hurt. It was then that I began to realise that it wasn't always going to be practical for me to light a candle whenever I felt that I needed to retreat within myself to escape the reality that overpowered me.

This was when I started to train myself to meditate without having to depend on the light of the flame. I was sure I wouldn't be able to do it though. For many years I had relied on candles, on the scents, and on the warm glow to diffuse my anxiety. But I knew that I had to try if I ever wanted to free myself from the crushing pressure of my life. In time I discovered that, as long as I continued to imagine in my mind the comforting sensations of the delicate flame and combined it with the memory of the sweet vanilla scent, I was able to remove myself from any moment and focus only on the inside of my mind. It has become one of the most important aspects of my existence. I can't imagine where I would be without meditation.

However, as time went by, it became a real challenge to maintain the harmony of my happy place. I have never had difficulty in being able to withdraw myself from my surroundings, but the upkeep of the space within my four walls has proved to be exhausting.

It used to look so beautiful. The floor was coated in a plush white carpet; it was free from dirt and stains, and it never wore away as I danced across it. A natural light always poured throughout my space, and even during the night it was never dark. The air was light and fresh, and it always smelled sweet and inviting. The walls themselves did not display their hideous brickwork, but instead were covered in cream coloured wallpaper that was almost velvet to the touch.

And then one day whilst I was skipping around within my walls I happened to trip over something. This was odd as, when I turned round, there was nothing on the floor. As I caught my toe though it must have snagged against the thick carpet, as I noticed that a small loop had appeared. I decided to leave the thread alone; I knew pulling at it would only make it worse.

But then it started to spread. I tried to avoid the rip in the carpet, but whenever I stepped it seemed to grow further and further, even if I was standing nowhere near that particular spot. Before I knew it, the rip traveled all the way to the edge of the back wall. It moved upwards as the wallpaper began to peel off to reveal the ugly surface behind it. Everything was falling apart and I couldn't stop it.

The next thing I knew, the air had become damp, making it difficult to breathe. The ground beneath me was coated in soil, and the walls were cold as they echoed their darkness all around me. I was trapped, frightened. I was still all on my own, but now I didn't like it.

I must remind myself though that, while I may be isolated and far away, I am still away from the cruelties of the outside world. It is dark, but I am thankful that I am not being attacked by the intrusive lights that try to burrow their way in.

I have grown to feel slightly more at ease within my surroundings. Ever since I was visited by Angel Ariana, I've noticed a different texture to the air. It is still thick, but as I inhale I can almost taste a light freshness, as if she had left part of her behind with me.

I wonder if there is something beyond this. Something beyond my own four walls. I know I am safe from others while I am here, but still I long to escape the dusty soil that lines the floor, and the darkness that makes me blind even to my immediate surroundings.

I decide to move myself back onto my hands and knees. I wonder if I am brave enough to move further without the light of my guardian angel here to protect me. I consider the possibility of crossing over to the other side of my walls.

I put my left hand out onto the ground in front of me. It nudges into one of the broken shards of rock. I draw it back quickly to escape the pain, before I attempt to ease it down again as I feel for a safer patch on the floor.

I begin to panic. What was I thinking? I can't do this on my own. I feel my breathing quicken in pace as my heart races. Something tells me that I cannot go on alone. I must not crawl further. As I place my right hand down, ready to give up, I feel something soft lying on the ground.

In the blackness of the space I am unable to see what it is, but I can feel the warmth of the mysterious object beneath my palm. I go to pick it up between my two fingers, and as I do so it starts to glow softly.

Now that it is illuminated, I can see exactly what it is: it's a feather! It looks identical to the feathers that cascade down to form Angel Ariana's wings. It spreads out full and luscious. Amongst its fresh white colour a gentle silver sparkle glistens as I turn it over.

I place the feather carefully in the palm of my hand, allowing its ends to point up towards the heavens. It appears to be made up of more tiny little fibers than I would ever be able to count. It feels fragile in my hand. I know I must protect it, but at the same time it seems to be made of such a great strength that it would be impossible for it to become damaged or destroyed at the grasp of a human hand.

I find myself leaning back into the security of the wall, ensuring I don't let go of my feather as I do so. As I continue to hold onto it, my hand starts to tingle. The sensation reminds me of pins and needles as it stretches down from the center of my palm right to my fingertips. This sensation begins to travel steadily up my right arm, and continues down my left until it reaches my fingers at the other side. It moves throughout me, and before I know it my whole body feels as though it is floating.

My eyelids become heavy all of a sudden. I close

them for a moment to rest them, making sure I don't let go of my feather. I concentrate as the bright white light of the feather begins to grow and emerge behind my eyes. As the light appears directly in my head, I start to feel as though I'm becoming detached from my body, as if my mind being transported somewhere else.

Chapter Fourteen

"Fiona!" Martin shouted as he stormed his way through to the bedroom. Fiona was lying in the middle of the bed, curled up with the white bed sheet wrapped tightly around her. "Fiona, wake up!" He tugged at the sheet so that it pulled away from her.

Fiona drew her legs in closer towards her as the sudden chill of the bitter evening air engulfed her. She opened a single sleepy eye to see what had disturbed her sleep. She glanced up to see her husband standing over her. "Martin, what's the matter?"

He threw the crumpled up piece of paper at her from where he had been clutching onto it in a balled fist. "This! This is the matter!"

Fiona pushed her hands onto the thin mattress to ease her tired body up so that she was sitting upright. "What's this?" she asked, fighting back a yawn.

She picked up the crumpled ball from where it had landed in front of her and teased it open. She recognised her words instantly. "It's just a poem. Martin," she replied, confused.

"It's just a poem?" He laughed sarcastically. "Just a poem?! Don't fool me, woman! Who is this *poem* about?"

"What? Martin, please stop shouting. It's the middle of the night, and I have such a horrific headache." She rubbed her forehead with her eyes closed for a moment as she tried to concentrate.

"Fiona, tell me who the poem is about." He emphasised each word as he spat them out at her in anger.

Fiona couldn't remember ever seeing Martin like this before. He had been annoyed in the past, usually over something that had happened at work or when the children down the street were throwing sticks again, but she had never seem him in such a rage as this. She found herself becoming quite frightened. She thought for a moment before answering, wondering whether or not the truth would be the best. "It's about Augusta," she decided.

"It's about...sorry, what? Who?!" It wasn't the answer Martin had been expecting. He was struggling to catch his breath now as he stood beside the bed, his eyes wide and angry. She wasn't making any sense.

Fiona looked wearily at her husband as he towered over her. "The poem is about Augusta Leigh, Martin. Look, please just come to bed and we can talk..."

"No, Fiona! Who is this Augusta Leigh? Where does this woman live?! I assume it's a woman, or a man with a very unfortunate name!" His spoke quickly, not really sure of what he was actually saying as he tried to arrange the thoughts that scattered around his mind.

"Augusta Leigh was Lord Byron's half-sister, Martin. The inspiration came to me when I was reading his work, that's all." Fiona yawned, longing to go back to sleep as her rapid thinking was tiring her out further.

"Oh, you and that bloody poet!"

Fiona chose to ignore that remark. "Byron was madly in love with her but she had married somebody else. He was heartbroken. Distraught. It's suggested that they did have a child together though, a little girl named Elizabeth Medora..."

"That's incest." He was disgusted by such a thought.

"Yes, Martin." Fiona had perked up a little with the chance she'd been given to talk about her favourite poet. She tried to carry on. "Byron's own marriage..."

"You're lying," Martin interrupted.

Fiona was taken aback by this accusation. "What?"

"I don't believe a word of it. None of that's true."

"It is, Martin. I swear!" Fiona was growing increasingly confused. She couldn't work out whether Martin was suggesting that Augusta Leigh didn't exist, or that she wasn't the real subject of her lines.

"Tell me who the poem is really about, Fiona. I demand that you tell me the truth *now*!" His last word echoed around the room before it bounced around inside Fiona's head. "Fiona McGonnell, who is it that you're so in love with that you had to write this...

this..." His heart was pounding, the blood circulating around his body at a rapid pace.

"Martin, please stop being silly. You know it's you that I love." She couldn't believe he was accusing her of spending her time thinking about another. He had always trusted her.

She stretched out of bed and turned to the door. "I'm going to get a drink of water." She almost felt as if she was asking him for permission to do so. She slid her bare feet into her flimsy shoes from where she'd left them at the entrance to the bedroom, before padding her way through to the kitchen, still tired and fighting for energy. Martin grabbed the sheet of paper from where Fiona had left it on the bed and bounded through behind her.

Fiona picked up the bowl from the kitchen counter. She was considering nipping back through to the bedroom to grab her cardigan to cover her naked arms; the bitter autumn air was going to pinch at her delicate skin. She eventually decided to be brave and just go out in her nightdress. She knew she would only be gone for a few minutes, and she wanted to get back to bed as quickly as possible. It frightened her to see Martin in such an angry state.

"Wait!" Martin demanded just as Fiona was about to open the front door. "I need to know who the poem is about." It didn't matter that she had tried to explain this to him several times now. He didn't seem to be listening to her. He was breathless, the rage harsh and overpowering in the back of his voice.

"Martin," she sighed. "I have explained this already to you." She tried to sustain a sense of calm in her own voice, but her own heart had started to pick up pace. She couldn't get her head around the fact that she was feeling fear towards her husband.

"You don't expect me to believe that rubbish about the incest? I don't believe anybody would choose to sleep with their sister!"

"Half-sister." She regretted correcting Martin the second the words had left her mouth. She didn't even know why she had said it. It wasn't going to make a difference.

"Excuse me?"

"I'm sorry, Martin. I really need to go and fill this up before the night grows even colder." Fiona turned to the door and opened it with her free hand, allowing the chill of the breeze to whip around the kitchen. It shocked both of them for a second; neither had expected the wind to be so strong. She crossed out into the open night air, and walked around the back of the house to where the main water pump was located.

Martin paused for a second. His mind had become empty for a moment, vacant of all thought. He was void of all emotions, if only just for a second, with his feet rooted to the spot. Then, as soon as his attention clicked back to reality, something inside of him snapped. It was a sensation like none other that he had ever felt before. All of the anger, all of the hatred that he had ever locked away, suddenly rushed to the surface. Any negative emotions he had suppressed over the years had decided that they no longer wanted to remain hidden away. His heart was aching at the thought of his wife loving another, but his mind was enraged. He decided that something had to be done. Not thinking clearly, he let his surge of emotions take control.

He lunged his weight forwards and raced out the

door. Just before he left, he reached out his right hand, an action that was carried out almost subconsciously, and grabbed hold of the little knife that Fiona had used to sharpen her pencil before writing the poem earlier that day. She'd left it on the counter, forgetting to put it away. He clutched onto the tool's weak handle as he charged his way through the bitter air. He turned the corner, stopping to a halt when he saw Fiona crouched down on the floor.

She didn't notice him as he stood there silently, his breathing deep as he watched her. He studied the way she swirled the water around in the bowl as she pumped it out. If only for a second, Martin almost forgot about the rage that had bubbled up inside of him. This was his wife he was talking about. She would never hurt him.

And then his attention was brought back to the poem. He turned her words around and around in his head, trying to make sense of it. Black ice. Forbidden love. Sinful wrong. He knew he was right, he had to be. She was in love with somebody else, and for that she had to be punished.

He took a step towards her, the pressure of his boot snapping a twig in half as he pressed down on it. Fiona jumped, startled by the sudden noise. It caused her to completely knock over the bowl, spilling the water everywhere as it landed upside down. "Martin," she spoke softly, as she caught her breath after the scare. "I didn't see you there."

He didn't respond. His eyes were fixed, staring directly through her. He breathed heavily.

Fiona looked down and noticed the knife clenched in Martin's fist. She gasped. She instantly became frozen to the spot, unable to move from the patch of grass upon which she was kneeling. Her arms locked by her side. "Martin? Why are you carrying a knife?" She knew it wasn't a sensible question. She didn't expect an answer.

She couldn't understand what was going on. "Is this about the poem, Martin? I promise you it's not about anybody I know!" Her words were frantic. A panic rose from within her.

Martin's breathing became more fierce as he took another step towards Fiona. He moved closer, making each step stronger than the previous. Fiona knew she had to do something, but her confusion barricaded her actions. She struggled to assess the situation as her mind raced. She had never before felt in danger at the hands of her husband. What was she supposed to do?

She had to run.

As Martin drew the gap between them another step closer, Fiona tried to stand up. She stumbled backwards, narrowly avoiding tripping over the water bowl as she did so, and ran. She ran right around the back of the house. She ran around to the other side, to the front. She couldn't carry on to the front door. She didn't know why, but she knew she must escape her husband. She couldn't go back into the house. It wasn't safe.

She ran, and she kept on running, but she knew her weary legs would be no match for Martin's powerful strides.

She could hear him booming up behind her as she made her way up the path. She tried not to slip on the wet mud as she clambered along amongst the slippery leaves, taking her further and further away from the house. She was crying now. The tears were falling down her cheeks. She had lost all control. She was beginning to wonder if she'd escape the situation. She had no idea how she could calm Martin down. An instant fear of her husband had been born within her that she knew she would never be able to forget.

Fiona's heart raced as she came to the bridge. She paused and turned round; Martin was only a few seconds behind her. She had to continue running. She couldn't turn back. There was no other option.

She began to cross over the cobbles of the bridge. Above her she could see the rich black of the night sky. It was a comfort to her in the moment. Each star that twinkled seemed to be filled with more love than Fiona could ever imagine. The moon shone down on her as if showering her with warmth and protection.

She had nearly made it to the end of the bridge. But as it curved to stretch across the river she lost her balance. She tripped as she caught the front of her thin shoe in between two of the cobbles. She fell with a thud down onto the solid, cold surface of the bridge. She tried to ignore the pain as it grazed against her knees. She knew she didn't have time to worry about the shooting agony that now engulfed her right arm. Struggling with the last of her energy, she managed to pull herself to her feet. But it was too late.

Martin grabbed hold of Fiona and pinned her against the wall of the bridge. Beneath the bridge, Fiona could see the rapid waters of the Don as it raced down the stream. She knew that if she fell in, if she was pushed over, her life would be over. "Martin, please," she begged, in a quiet whimper.

But Martin wasn't paying attention. He had lost

control of his own emotions as he raised his hand high into the air. Fiona's eyes flickered between the hurt in his eyes and the object in his hand, before she watched, helpless, as Martin plunged his hand down firmly onto Fiona's chest. Everything seemed to happen in slow motion as the knife pierced through her pale skin. She let out a shrilled scream.

Shaking, Martin let go of his wife. Her body slid down to the floor at his feet. What had he done? He looked down at the knife in his hand. It seemed to be glued to him as he stared at it, unable to take his eyes away from the crimson droplets of blood that now glistened on its surface. His stomach churned wildly. He was sure he was going to throw up. In a panic, he flung the knife over the bridge, letting it disappear into the murky depths of the river.

He dropped to his knees by Fiona's side. She lay completely still, silent. Her eyes remained only half open. As he fumbled for her pulse, Martin found that she was still alive. She was still breathing, if only just.

"Fiona, I..." he began. He didn't know what he wanted to say. He tried to get his head around what had just happened, but his mind remained blank. "I'm sorry," he eventually managed.

He held her in his arms as he hugged her tightly towards his chest. He didn't know what had come over him. Was it jealousy? He had feared that she was in love with somebody else, with another man. He didn't want to lose her. He couldn't let anybody else have her. She was his wife. *His* wife. He hadn't meant to cause her any harm.

"I should have believed you. I'm so sorry. " He was sobbing now. He knew that no words, no excuses, would ever be enough. "I'm so sorry, Fiona!"

As he held her, he could feel the life in his wife's body begin to drain away. Fiona managed to open her eyes a little, as she looked up at Martin. She knew it would be the last time she would be able to look into the eyes of her husband. Just as her spirit was about to step outside of her body, she managed to find the strength to whisper her final words to her husband. She spoke something that she had always meant, something that she knew she would always feel deep within her. As she whispered her last breath to Martin, it transformed his sobs into an uncontrollable wail.

She gasped her final breath and uttered, "I love you."

Chapter Fifteen

Without warning, my attention snaps back to my own surroundings. I've curled into a ball again, my back arched as I lean closer into the wall. I sob into myself as I become overwhelmed with emotions. I feel certain that somebody has ripped my heart right out from inside me. The pain is physical. It is impossible. I cannot find any ability to move. My chest tightens as I stay frozen where I sit. It feels as though somebody has sliced a dagger right through me, turning it and churning it as they chop my heart up into pulp. But the ache is not just physical. My heart beats wildly, as if yearning for something it once used to feel. It searches for a love of something, a love of someone. It cries in its own loneliness. I try to fight the agony as I double over in pain. I begin to retch.

I manage to find the strength to take a deep

breath, filling my lungs to try and soothe my heart. I open my eyes to find that I am no longer in darkness, but instead I am shielded by a beautiful white light. I look up to see that Angel Ariana is smiling down at me. I return this with my own weak smile, comforted by the presence of my guardian angel in front of me.

She has wrapped her wings around me, as if creating a circle to lock in her protective warmth. I am encased in her feathers, which are spread out full now. They stretch right out as they show off their delicate fibers. I suddenly remember my own feather and turn around to look for it. It has disappeared.

Angel Ariana can sense what I am looking for, and tells me not to worry. She explains that my feather doesn't exist physically now as I had allowed it to become at one with my own body. The words sound magical as she utters them softly to me.

Her wings look much longer than before. They almost touch the floor now as they stretch down. They completely avoid the dirt that has taken over my walls though, remaining fresh and white and untarnished. They are pure.

As my guardian angel nods towards me, I can feel that she is beginning to absorb some of the pain that had crippled me. My chest eases as Angel Ariana removes the invisible dagger that had punctured right through me. I am relieved when I am no longer doubled over from the torturous force. The physical pressures to my heart, and to my chest, have been lifted.

I whisper a weak thank you to Angel Ariana. She does not reply, but she continues to keep her wings wrapped around me. Though I am greatly thankful that she has removed my physical suffering, I wonder why I am still able to feel the emotional struggle. Why hasn't she taken this away with the rest of my pain?

I am able to sit upright now, my back once more pressed against the wall as I start to breathe a little more easily. I've managed to calm down and stop myself from sobbing, but it's still a struggle to completely fight the tears back. My emotions are still torn. I cannot work out whether or not any of them are my own any more.

Angel Ariana looks right into my eyes now. Her own eyes are so soft and loving, but they seem a lot brighter than they did before. They are still full of all the colours of the world, but now they also seem to sparkle spectacularly with a dazzling gold. I've never seen anything so magical before.

My angel tells me that I'm struggling to suppress the emotions I have no control over as I must first come to terms with them. I say nothing now, but look up at her with hope in my heart. I know she can see right into me. I know she will be able to feel the ache in my soul.

Angel Ariana speaks to me now. I don't understand what she says to me, but I take her words on board. She tells me that I'm growing, and that I feel small within my walls as I remain on the floor wrapped safely inside her wings. I still have a way to go before I am ready. I have no control over the way I feel. I know the outside world is right behind me. I feel safe with Angel Ariana right next to me, but I am always aware of the many dangers that lie so close to me. I wonder if I can ever be saved.

She begins to spread her wings back out. She uncurls them cautiously from around me. As she does so, I don't feel scared like I had expected to when the darkness from outside her wings began to make itself known. Instead, I actually feel just as secure as I was when I was wrapped within her. The air around me feels a lot warmer now than it used to. The weight of the anxiety that had spread throughout me begins to drift away.

I watch my guardian angel take a step back away from me. She cannot be any more than two meters away, but there is once again darkness all around the room as she takes her light with her. However, the pool of white around her feet seems much brighter now. It appears fluid, as if it is trying to grow.

As I concentrate on this light that sits beneath her, the air begins to fill with the same relaxing sounds that her presence has previously brought to me. I am certain that I recognise the tune of the delicate music, yet I still cannot establish what it is. It comforts me into a state of utter calm. The sounds are still quite faint, but I can hear it. Angel Ariana doesn't flinch as it begins to play a little louder, more strong. It's such a beautiful sound. It seems to be coming directly from within both Angel Ariana and myself now.

She spreads her wings wide by her side, stretching them out so that they bend backwards slightly. They are sparkling, each feather lit up with its own unique silver twinkle. She smiles at me. It's a broad smile, and as I watch her I am overcome with a sense of urgency. Something is about to happen, I can feel it.

Chapter Sixteen

Maggie hunched inwards, shaking as her legs struggled to support her exhausted body. She kept her eyes to the ground, darting them back and forth as if wishing for a trap door to suddenly appear to offer her an escape. Peter's fist was clenched tightly around the top of her arm, making sure that she was unable to move. Unable to escape.

He breathed heavily, almost panting. Every time he exhaled, the stench of alcohol spread itself across Maggie's face as he leaned closer. "Do you know what you're going to do for me?"

Maggie didn't answer. She couldn't. Her mind was frantically trying to find a way out.

"You, Margaret," he paused to swallow a burp, "are going to bring him back for me." As he spoke, his breath blew at the side of her neck, forcing the damage he'd done to Maggie's hair to itch away at her skin. As she wiggled to escape the reminder of her suffering, Peter tightened his grip.

She could feel the blood rushing to the top of her arm as his meaty fingers clamped around her fragile skin. She felt sick. Every part of her body wanted to retch in fear. She tried to focus her mind on whatever it was that Peter had just said to her, but she couldn't remember his words.

"Did you hear me Margaret?"

She shook her head. She knew immediately that it wasn't the answer Peter was looking for.

"Perhaps you need to start paying more attention to your husband then, Margaret." His voice was a lot calmer than Maggie had expected it to sound, a lot more soft. She found it threatening, as it offered her an uncertainly over what Peter was thinking. He continued to speak slowly to her. "If you had listened to me the first time, Margaret, then you would have heard what I had said. I'm offering you the chance to bring him back to me."

Bring who back? Maggie was unable to comprehend what Peter was saying to her.

"He was such a sweet little boy." Peter released his grip from Maggie's arm as he leaned over the table to pick up her scrapbook. He seemed to take more care of handling it this time as he held it open at the page displaying Thomas's baby photo. Peter ran his finger around the edges of the picture, stroking it. "Look at him, Margaret."

She kept her eyes to the ground. She didn't need to look at the photo to feel the ache in her heart that had remained there for the last sixteen years.

"Look at him!" Peter's voice was raised again as

he thrust the scrapbook down in front of Maggie's face. She tried to fight the tears back as she was forced to look at the image of her baby boy. She had always blamed herself for what had happened. Peter had told her it was her fault, too. Who else could he have blamed? She tried to flood her mind with all the happy memories she had shared with her son, but each one rested in the shadow of his absence.

"Oh, stop your bloody crying. We can't do this if you're going to blubber all over the place."

Maggie sniffed as she attempted to control her sobbing.

"Daddy's doing this for you, my precious boy," Peter spoke to the photo. "You're too young to watch though, wee Thomas. We'll see you later son." He smirked to himself, one side of his lip raised higher than the other. He closed the scrapbook to shield his son's eyes, before dropping it back onto the table.

He was about to drink the last of the vodka in his glass, but as he went to reach for it he couldn't seem to take his eyes away from the cover of the scrapbook. He stopped his hand to pick up the scrapbook again. He held it up, studying the display.

"She's hideous," he voiced. "She keeps staring at me. Who does she think she is? What is she even meant to be?!" Maggie could sense the anger rising again in Peter's voice. She wasn't sure if she preferred that to the sinister presence of his whispers. "Why would you draw such a stupid, ugly thing anyway? I mean, angels don't even exist."

She was an angel!

Why hadn't she realised that before? Suddenly she could see it now. The woman she had drawn on the bridge as a child, the woman she had seen in her dreams, had been an angel.

"I will not have my son overshadowed by some pathetic, childish little girl's drawing! You're such an idiot! A stupid, selfish, worthless idiot!" With each word Peter tore at the scrapbook. Each page shredded into little pieces. They fell to the floor, scattered. The angel's wings were crumpled. The prom photo had been ripped down the middle. Maggie's beautiful autumn leaf sat loose and unloved.

And there, right in the center of the torn scrapbook, Thomas's little face stared up at his parents, ripped in half.

As Peter's rage started to subside, the realisation of what he had just done suddenly hit him with force. "Thomas!" He crouched down to the floor and picked up the two pieces of the photo, holding one in each hand. "My beautiful little son." To both his surprise and Maggie's, he started crying. "Daddy didn't mean it. I'm so sorry, my son. Please forgive me!"

Maggie couldn't take her eyes away from the pile that now lay at her feet. All of her hard work, all of her memories. Gone. Ripped up and scattered, never to be restored.

Peter tried to position the photo back together and held it gently in his hands. He stroked his child's button nose, kissing it lightly before hugging it close to his chest. If only for a brief moment, he was alone in the world with his son. Nothing else mattered to him. Nobody else mattered.

As the aggression that was boiling inside of him began to overpower his sentiment, he rose up and placed the photo safely on the table, before turning to Maggie. "Look what you made me do!" He lifted his hand in the air, much higher than even he had intended to, and swung at Maggie's face. She didn't have time to turn her head. The blow hit her full force across her cheek and left eye, complete with a hollow cracking sound. Her reflexes told her to lift her hands to her face to try and calm the pain, but Peter snatched hold of her wrists and squeezed them. He gripped onto her tightly with his fists.

"You're a pathetic little bitch, Margaret." He slurred his words at her. She couldn't look at him. "Don't be so bloody ignorant! You look at your husband when he's talking to you!" Peter grabbed hold of her face and held it up close to his. He spat directly at her. "There's nothing worse than a woman who doesn't know how to obey her husband."

Maggie quivered. As she looked into Peter's eyes she knew she was looking now into the eyes of a stranger. This was not the man she had married.

He picked up the scissors again, sending shivers of panic right through Maggie.

"Peter..." She didn't know what she was trying to say. She didn't know what he was going to do. She realised she didn't know anything any more.

"Don't worry, Margaret. I'm not going to hurt you." He balanced the scissors in between his fingers for a second, before pressing the cold blade against Maggie's shoulder. He let it sit there for a moment, as if admiring the shape of the instrument. Maggie closed her eyes, too frightened to take anything in.

The scissors snipped.

The strap parted in two, loosening the dress as it sat around Maggie's chest. "You were lying to me, weren't you, Margaret?" He moved the scissors over to her other shoulder. "I know you bought this dress without asking me. All that rubbish you told to Lucy about finding it in your wardrobe was just a filthy, dirty lie. It makes you look like a common tart. It's disgusting. Hideous! You'll look better without it on, Margaret. Trust me."

The scissors snipped again.

Peter took care in placing the scissors down this time, his movements slower as he made sure he didn't set them anywhere near the photo of his son. He ran his hands softly up Maggie's bare arms. She drew her arms inwards at his touch. She couldn't bear the feeling of his skin against hers. She recoiled as he ran the tips of his fingers across the top of her bare chest.

"Come on." He spoke softly. Maggie continued to lean against the table, only half conscious of what Peter was saying to her.

"Move!" He flung her forward towards the door. She stumbled as she stood on the remains of her scrapbook, scattering them further across the floor. She wanted to scream out for help as Peter pushed her from behind, forcing her to move towards the hall, but she couldn't.

She could see the front door. It was only a few meters away. If she could just find the strength to run, the strength to break free from the prison he'd created for her.

Peter shoved her into the bedroom. Managing to regain her balance, Maggie froze to the spot for a second. She wanted to run, but she was too frightened to move.

Thunder rumbled through the night sky, stopping Peter in his tracks as he entered the room after her. "Stupid storm," he muttered, annoyed that it was getting in the way of his thoughts. "I know what we need." He turned his attention to the Hi-Fi that sat on top of the chest of drawers. He opened up the top to see what disc had been left inside before closing it, satisfied. As he hit the button to start playing the first track, an instrumental jazz song began to sound out of the speakers. He decided it would be perfect to drown out the intrusive thunderstorm that was brewing outside.

Maggie flinched as she felt Peter's arm grab hold of her waist from behind. His hands were like ice, penetrating through her skin and into her soul. Her dress fell down to her feet as Peter pulled at its fabric, leaving her exposed and vulnerable. With her heart racing, she listened to hear a faint metallic click.

His belt.

Thoughts began to zip through her mind as she forced herself to focus on the reality of her surroundings. She heard a soft thud come from behind her as Peter allowed his trousers to drop to the ground. They brushed against the backs of her ankles as he moved closer towards her. Maggie tried to work out what was happening. His hot breath was thick on the back of her neck as he moved closer towards her, fumbling with the clasp of her bra until it came undone.

He pulled her around so that she was facing him. Unable to look at him, she held her eyes tightly closed as she forced back her tears.

He used his weight to push her towards the bed, his naked chest pressed firmly against her fragile body. He bit kisses into her neck as he forced her backwards. He ran his hand up clumsily to the top of her thigh as he positioned himself on top of her, inside of her.

She was able to feel every part of her body drawing inwards as he pressed his clammy bare legs against her pale thighs. She was unable to move as he forced himself further down onto her. She tried to find the strength to cry out, but it was no use. Drained, she could do nothing but lie there and take his weight as he rocked his drunken body back and forth. She was too weak to fight it, too frail to speak. She could only whisper her cries as they remained inside her mind. No, Peter. Please, Peter.

Stop.

Chapter Seventeen

Every inch of my body aches. My feet are cold, painful and numb. The rough surface beneath me is sharp, intrusive. The air around me remains thick as it tries to suffocate me. I twitch my nose as I sniff back my tears. It smells foul, an overpowering stench of sweat and alcohol and torture. My skin begins to itch. It feels as though lots of tiny insects are crawling all over my body. I stand straight, still, my eyes closed. Rooted to the spot, I am unable to move.

There is silence all around me. Inside my walls lies only stillness. I'm cut off from the rest of the world. No sound can get in. No negative thoughts can pierce their way through. And yet my heart is racing. There is a fear moving all around me, smothering my entire body until my existence is coated in hatred and sorrow.

I am burning up. I can feel it in my cheeks, the blood rising into my face as it tries to demand its way out through my skin. There is an enormous pressure against my chest. It is stronger than any nightmare I have ever imagined. I struggle to breathe as I try to inhale rapidly. I wheeze as I fight my way through the anxiety.

I begin to find myself feeling light-headed, a symptom, I thought, of my inability to breathe properly. But then I can feel it traveling. My shoulders instantly start to feel free, without weight. The pressure from my chest is lifted. It's the most glorious feeling to be able to breathe again.

I try to open my eyes, but I cannot. The tension continues to be released around me. My arms are light by my sides. My legs and my feet become weightless. The physical pain has been lifted.

I'm finally able to open my eyes. Before me stands Angel Ariana. She says I needed to face something before we can continue. I know I shouldn't question why I must continue to ache, but I cannot understand it.

Her wings have curved towards me again. It is almost as if they are beckoning me forward. Between us appears the silver river of light I had previously admired. Only now it's a lot more sparkly than it was the first time. It shimmers.

I look at my guardian angel, confused.

She explains to me that she wants to show me something important. I was not supposed to enter such a state of panic before. I must pay full attention.

Pay attention to what? I ask Angel Ariana if she can explain to me what she means.

She tells me she needs me to turn around. I don't

know why I am being asked to do this, but I do as Angel Ariana has requested. I move slowly, turning my back away from the comforting glow of my angel, and instead forcing myself to stare into the darkness of the wall opposite.

I know she still stands behind me. The room is warm with her presence. I trust her, but the uncertainty of the space in front of me is threatening. I don't know what I am supposed to be looking at. I voice this to Angel Ariana, worried that I am supposed to be seeing something that I am unable to. She explains to me that I must have patience.

A few moments later, the wall in front of me lights up. The dark, cold space is replaced with a beautiful white light. It stretches itself across the entire length and height of where the previous dirty brick wall stood. I cannot stop myself from blinking for a moment to shield my eyes from its intensity. It is a dazzling, beautiful white. I am mesmerised.

My angel tells me that I must watch closely. She is about to show me something that will help me, and I am going to learn from it. I nod as I stand in front of her, unable to take my eyes away from the bright screen that has appeared before me.

Suddenly, the white light flickers. The screen displays a fuzzy grey image, as if somebody had just put an old VHS tape into a player, the video crawling to life. The tape takes a couple of seconds to kick in, continuing to flicker a few times before it launches into action. As I watch, I find myself losing all sense of my surroundings. I can no longer detect the walls around me, and the air has become so thin and pure than I am unable to taste it. An image finally appears on screen. I stare at it as it begins to unfold.

Chapter Eighteen

He wiped his sleeve across his face has he tried to mop up the tears that had now smeared their salty tracks down his cheeks. He sniveled, trying to pull himself together. He sat uneven on the cobbles, the night sky bellowing down on him from the heavens. He gazed up as if searching for an answer, seeking out help. The stars stared back at him, drilling guilt right through Martin's soul.

He turned his attention back to Fiona. She lay there, still and silent in his arms. Her body rested motionless, her heart stolen of its life. What was he supposed to do now? His mind raced with thoughts. He looked down at the patch of blood that had oozed through Fiona's nightdress, the same blood that had stained and sank into his hands. A crimson reminder of his eternal guilt. He knew he would not be able to escape what he had done.

Or could he?

His mind worked in overdrive as an idea started to emerge from within the confusion. He wasn't sure if it was going to work or not, but he had no other option. He had to give it a try.

He pushed himself up off the cobbled ground. Bending his knees slightly, he scooped up Fiona's body and held her to his chest to shield her from the fierce weather. Now that they were no longer sheltered by the walls of the bridge, the winds attacked into them sharply as it seemed to speed from all directions. Martin glanced around, making sure nobody was able to see them.

Through the darkness he carried Fiona back to their house. With every footstep on the way he tried to be completely silent, but every crunch of gravel, and every twig that snapped, echoed through the air as if sending out an alarm to alert all of Balgownie about what he had done.

He continued through to the bedroom so that he could lie Fiona down on their bed. She lay peacefully on her back as Martin drew the bed sheet around her. He made sure it was wrapped snugly under her feet, before tucking it beneath her arms to stop her from feeling the chill of the night.

From under the bed he pulled out a small attaché case. It was rather battered and worn, having belonged to Fiona's father many years ago. William had managed to save up all of his birthday money along with any loose change visiting relatives would give him throughout his teenage years so that when he got his first job he would be able to buy himself a brand new case. It was his pride and joy. He would take it everywhere with him, displaying it proudly. But when the handle started to come loose he decided to save it only for special occasions. Once a hole had developed in it though, he decided it was time to retire it for good, and stuffed it in a drawer somewhere out of sight. Years later, Fiona had discovered it whilst cleaning out whatever few belongings he had come into possession of over the years. She had remembered seeing the bag in her childhood, and knew how much it had meant to William. She decided to patch up the hole in his memory, before laying the case to rest under the bed.

Martin stuffed his underwear from the drawers beside his bed into the case. He glanced over at Fiona every few seconds nervously as he continued to bundle a few other bit and pieces together. He struggled with the clasp as he tried to fasten it, only just managing to get it to close.

He had left his jacket in the kitchen earlier on. It was when he walked through and went to pick it up from where he'd hung it on the back of the chair that he remembered the blood on his hands. He began to panic again. From under the kitchen sink he brought out a hard brush used for scrubbing his boots clean. He fished around until he found a small metal dish, inside which sat the grubby remnants of what was once a clean white bar of soap.

He left through the front door and made his way to the water pump round the back. He was terrified that somebody would be watching out of their window, wondering what he was up to at such an early hour in the morning. He released some of the water, trying not to let his mind focus on the bowl that had tipped over when he had crept up on Fiona.

It still lay upside down on the grass beside him, a reminder of what he had done.

Under the cold drips he began scrubbing his hands furiously. He scraped at his knuckles with the hard bristles of the brush. He attempted to make the scraps of soap lather, but his best efforts were not good enough. He scrubbed and he rinsed, until only the slightest flecks of Fiona's essence remained underneath his fingernails.

His hands were now freezing cold from the water. He returned to the house, drying them on the kitchen rag as he escaped the bitterness of the outdoors. He paused at the kitchen door, before continuing back through to the bedroom. He hovered at the side of the bed.

He looked at his wife. A single tear rolled down his left cheek as he fought to block out the reality of his actions. He leaned forward and kissed her on the forehead. "I'll always love you," he whispered softly to her.

Martin picked up the attaché case and headed out of the bedroom. He couldn't find the strength in him to look at his wife one last time. Instead, he turned his back on her as she lay there, and continued on until he crossed back through the front door and into the open air outside. Behind him he closed the front door gently so as not to disturb anybody. He looked up at the sky one more time, before studying his surroundings. Even the twinkling of the stars failed to light up the darkness of that particular night sky. He turned his attention to the bridge as he started up the path.

His stomach turned as he crossed over the cobbles. He could hear the water running rapidly beneath him. It seemed to be shouting at him, accusing him. It was aware of his guilt. As he walked across he put his hand in his pocket. It collided with something. He pulled the object out to investigate. He'd forgotten that he'd hastily stuffed Fiona's lines in there before he...

Before he...

No, he was unable to finish his own thought.

He read her words again. His heart sank as his eyes filled up with tears. He had loved her. He was sure she had loved somebody else. Now she could not love anybody, and it was all his fault. He leaned over the edge of the bridge, and let the piece of paper fall down into the water. It lay on top of the river for a brief second, floating delicately on the surface, before the current engulfed it and dragged it down into the mysterious forbidden depths.

Martin carried on walking over the bridge, and turned the corner out of sight, never to return to Balgownie.

Chapter Nineteen

The screen has disappeared. My walls have returned to their previous state. I stand here in complete darkness.

Angel Ariana beckons for me to turn around. As I do this, my movements are cautious so that I don't stumble over. When I face her, I sense that she has grown brighter somehow. She appears even more glorious than before. She explains to me that the man in the vision was never seen again. Nobody on this earthly plane knew where he went, and few people thought to search for him. He was able to get away with what he had done.

I feel my heart sink in my chest. The poor woman! She couldn't escape. It was too late for her. Time had run out. As I stand there in front of my guardian angel, I begin to feel an ache in my stomach.

It starts out as a small knot, uncomfortable and quite inconvenient. But then it grows. It develops into a much stronger, more powerful agony, until I am able to stand it no longer.

I clutch my hands to my stomach. I look up into Angel Ariana's eyes and ask her what's going on. This is the pain that the woman had felt, she tells me. She had been forced to suffer before she passed away.

I'm sure I'm going to throw up. The ache becomes impossible. I need to sit down, but I am unable to find the strength to do so.

I am confused when I am told that it is not just the suffering of the woman that I am being allowed to feel. The hurt is that of her child's too.

She was with child.

As I realise this, Angel Ariana slowly draws the pain out of me until I find that I am able to stand myself upright again with a little more ease. It was not only one life that had been taken, but two. I put my hands to my face as I begin to cry. I cannot stop thinking about the poor defenseless baby. How horrible it was that it had to suffer at the hands of its own father.

Angel Ariana informs me that it was a little girl.

I am overcome with sadness. I weep for the little daughter who never had the chance to say hello to her mummy and daddy. I cry for the small child who was never given a chance at life. I mourn for the soul whose life was over before it even had begun.

Angel Ariana looks at me still. Her eyes are kind, but there is a firmness to them too. She speaks to me, tells me that nobody's path is fixed. Courses can be altered, but actions must be taken for this to happen. Decisions must be made before changes can occur.

She tells me I must be strong.

I listen to what she says to me. I try to process it. I understand there is great importance in her words. Something is being asked of me. My guardian angel needs me to do something. Action must be taken.

I must be strong.

Chapter Twenty

She hugged onto the duvet as she drew it closer to her body. A stream of the morning sun trickled its way in through the slight gap in the parting of the bedroom curtains. She stared at the wall in front of her, her eyes fixed on one blank, emotionless spot.

She hadn't been able to sleep, nor did she have the strength to get up in the middle of the night to seek out some warm pyjamas to protect her from the harshness of the night. Peter had laid beside her with his back to her, as he snored through to the morning. She tugged at the duvet so that it was wrapped closer to her face, and curled herself tightly into a ball.

She had cried herself to sleep, her silent sobs working to soothe her mind, if only slightly. She winced as she moved her body, a bruise on her right arm pressing uncomfortably into a loose spring in the mattress.

Maggie had listened as the alarm clock on Peter's mobile phone had sounded. She heard him heave his weight out of the bed and cross over to the floor where he had left the phone in his trouser pocket. He turned the alarm off, and headed to the bathroom.

She listened as the toilet flushed. She followed the sounds of his feet as he made his way through to the kitchen, clicked on the kettle, spooned out two teaspoons of coffee granules into a mug.

The kettle clicked. He filled the mug, stirred the coffee. He found his usual seat on the sofa and turned on the television. The breakfast news programme drowned out the sound of Peter gulping down the hot liquid. He turned off the TV, burped. Maggie listened as he brushed his teeth. She heard him fiddle with his electric shaver as he attempted to make himself look more presentable. He returned to the bedroom, opened the wardrobe door. He pulled out a shirt, a pair of trousers. He fished out some clean underwear, changed his socks.

She listened to the beeps of his phone as he punched a text message into the keypad. He clicked send. He slipped on his jacket, jangling his pocket to make sure he had his keys. He headed for the front door. He walked out, closed it behind him.

Maggie heard the car engine start up. He drove away, out of his parking spot. She lay in bed in the silence, alone.

The air was thick with his scent. Her thighs were marked red where he had clawed at her. She tried to ignore this, and to ignore her surroundings.

Her own mobile sounded from the living room, indicating that she had received a new text message.

Maggie took this as a blessing, allowing her the strength to leave the bed; she was never able to ignore her phone as she always feared some sort of emergency. She managed to force herself up so that she was sitting on the edge of the bed. She perched there for a moment with her head in her hands. She clasped the back of her neck as she felt the tufts of her hair in its uneven bob. She sniffed and wiped at her eyes, trying to stop herself from crying. Her eyes were stinging from the tears. Inhaling deeply, she leaned over the bottom of the bed and fished out a grey night shirt she'd left on the chair at the side. After pulling this over her head to allow her a little warmth and dignity, she gathered her strength and made her way through the cold morning house to retrieve her phone.

The message was from Lucy, thanking Maggie for last night. She had had a great time and was wondering if Maggie would like to go for a coffee later.

Maggie read the text a few times. She considered replying, but something told her to wait before responding. She rested her phone on the table, knocking her hand against the photo of her son that still sat there. She cast her eyes at the torn shreds of her precious scrapbook, and at the remains of her lovely long hair as they sat disordered across the floor.

She couldn't live like this any longer.

She needed something to drown out the haunting silence of the flat. She headed for her bedroom and turned her focus to the Hi-Fi. She pressed the button to begin playing the disc, forgetting what was inside the player. As the squeal of a saxophone filled the air around her, she flung her hand on top of the machine to stop it. She held onto her stomach as she tried not to throw up, the memories of the music from last night recreating in her mind.

She threw the disc onto the bed and rummaged among the collection of CDs that sat to the side. Eventually, she found what she was looking for. She placed it into the player and activated the first track. Suddenly, the sweet Irish sounds of Celtic Woman began to fill the room. The angelic harmonies had worked on relaxing Maggie's mind for many years. She hoped it would still be effective.

She made her way through to the bathroom, where she stopped to look into the mirror. She had to bite her lip to stop herself from bursting into tears again. Black tracks of mascara-stained tears ran down her cheeks. Her blonde hair no longer bounced as she moved her head. There was a mark across her face from where Peter's hand had collided with her cheek. She could still feel his fingers striking hot across her skin, scratching at her and demanding her attention. Her face tingled and itched as she thought about it.

She opened up the bathroom cabinet and pulled out a pack of face wipes. Teasing one out, she began to remove the damage that was now smeared across her face. She watched in the mirror as she wiped at her skin. Some problems were easier to remove than others.

She rinsed her face with cold water from the tap before dabbing her skin dry with a clean towel. She studied the tiredness that emerged around her eyes, the bags beneath her lower lashes growing greater as each day went by. She pulled a small black bag out of the cupboard, from which she plucked out a bottle of foundation. Using the tips of her fingers she lightly dabbed at her face with the foundation, blending it in evenly to try and make her look a little more presentable. She swept a mascara wand over her lashes, and finished with a dab of nude lipstick on her lips. It wasn't much, but it helped.

A power ballad began to sound from the bedroom as she re-entered it. From her wardrobe she reached for a pair of dark jeans and slipped them on. She discarded her night shirt and exchanged it for a loose t-shirt fitted with a cartoon image of a cat and a mouse. She brushed her hair out, and managed to scrape what Peter had allowed her to keep into a small ponytail. She assured herself that it didn't look too bad once she'd tied it back. It would soon grow back out.

On top of the wardrobe sat a black suitcase. Stretching up, Maggie was just about able to reach it to pull it down, throwing it on top of the bed. She zipped it open to find that it was empty, just as she had hoped.

Almost on autopilot, she pulled clothes from their hangers and folded them quickly into the suitcase. She emptied her drawer out, managing to fit everything in without having to force the zip. For the first time in her life, she was thankful for the fact that she didn't own very much.

There was just enough room left for the painting that hung on the wall. She unhooked the Monet landscape and placed it gently on top of her clothes. She ran her finger along the bridge, before closing the suitcase.

She glanced at the purple dress on the floor, deciding to leave it there where it belonged as she headed back to the living room. She fetched the broom from where it stood between the kitchen wall and the fridge, and began sweeping up the living room floor. As she bundled it all into the bin bag, she had to repeatedly remind herself that the memories that rested within the heart could never truly be forgotten. She would always treasure them in the place that it meant the most.

Returning to the bedroom, she switched off the Hi-Fi system and placed the disc back in its case. She clutched onto it as she returned to the side of the living room table and picked up the pieces of the photo. "You'll always be with me, Thomas," she spoke softly to the picture of her son. "I'll never forget you." She folded the two fragments over and slid them into the back pocket of her jeans. She placed her phone into her other pocket, and bent down to pick up her handbag from where she'd left it the previous evening.

She carried her handbag over to the shelf in the corner of the room and fished for Wollstonecraft's *A Vindication of the Rights of Woman*. She slid it into her handbag to take with her. It had helped her so far. She hoped it would help her further as she took this terrifying step.

Maggie returned to the bedroom and picked up her jacket from next to her suitcase. She slipped her arms into it and fastened up its buttons. She knew it would be a bitter autumn morning outside.

She stood for a moment looking down at her hand. Her wedding band hadn't left her finger since the day Peter had placed it there over twenty years ago. She turned it around a few times. As she did so, her entire marriage – the only existence she had ever really known – ran through her mind. Giving it a slight tug, she slipped the ring off, taking her engagement ring with it, and placed them on top of the chest of drawers next to Peter's phone charger.

She reached back into her trouser pocket for her phone. Pressing the menu button, she pulled up the text she had received from Lucy. She typed in a reply before hitting the icon to send it: *I'm coming over. Put the kettle on. Love Maggie x*

She returned her phone, and proceeded to lift the suitcase from the bed. She carried it with her handbag through into the hall. Her movements were slow as she tried to take in her surroundings. She had lived here for so many years. Was she really ready to do this? Could she really walk away from everything?

She thought about Peter's fists as he grabbed onto her. She thought about the cold blade of the scissors as he pressed it against her skin. She felt the scars on her arms and the scratches on her thighs caused by Peter's fingernails.

Yes, she could do this.

Turning the handle of the front door, she pulled it open. As she took a deep breath, she walked out, dragging the suitcase over the door frame. She fiddled for the keys in the bottom of her bag as she reminded herself to continue to breathe. She inhaled deeply to fill her lungs with air.

She turned the key in the lock and paused. Aware that she was beginning to doubt herself, she swiftly pulled the key out of the lock and opened the letter box before throwing the keys through. She heard them clatter as they landed on the wooden flooring. She didn't need them. She had everything she wanted to take with her. Anything else would only fill her with the bitter memories she longed to forget. Turning her back, she made for the building's main exit. There was no turning back.

She was free.

Chapter Twenty One

I stand facing Angel Ariana. She is glowing incredibly bright now, the golden light around her sparkling strong. I almost reach to cover my eyes for a moment, but they start to adjust. Her wings are spread long and wide. Each feather seems to be dancing in its own little breeze, swaying gently as the white shimmers and dazzles with its beautiful silver decoration.

She asks me to move closer towards her. I become anxious; I have never stood so close to my guardian angel before. She understands that I am worried. She tells me not to be afraid. I have nothing to be concerned about. I am in the hands of the angels. I am safe.

I move carefully, fearing that I will approach her too quickly, or move more closely than she has asked of me. After I have taken three steps, there exists only a short distance between us. If I were to reach out my hand, I am sure that my arm would stretch far enough for me to be able to touch her. But my arms remain down by my sides.

She asks me to put my hands in the air, not too far out but keeping them close to my chest. I do as I am asked, and watch as Angel Ariana does the same. Her hands are directly opposite mine now. Between us there grows a beautiful warmth. It makes me feel secure, protected. I know I am loved.

I almost cannot believe my eyes when the light appears between us. Running straight from Angel Ariana's hands and straight across to mine is a beam of white light. It is the brightest, most pure white I have ever seen. It's much stronger than the light that sits in a pool around my angel's feet. It is far greater than the white of the screen that took over one of my walls.

My hands tingle all over. The sensation is pleasant as it coats every fiber of my body. I become overwhelmed, unsure of what I am feeling.

Angel Ariana explains that she is removing my emotional pain. It is just like she did earlier when I was faced with physical difficulties, only she tells me that this takes a lot more energy and is much more challenging to do as she is working more closely with my soul.

As the light between us fades, she lowers her hands back down, and I find myself doing the same. I am too much in awe to speak. As I stand there silently, unable to make a sound, I can faintly hear a sweet sound floating through the air once more.

As it grows closer towards me, I become more aware of what it is. The beautiful notes of the organ are familiar to me, the gentle solo from the violin that reaches right into the soul, I have heard before.

I can see Angel Ariana is smiling at me, watching as I listen. The sound increases, allowing me to hear it much more clearly now. A smile stretches across my own face as I finally recognise what the tune is.

I can recall first hearing the song as a child when my mother took me to see the musical *Carousel* at the theatre. I'd fallen in love with the show, and have always listened to the soundtrack ever since I was a little girl. I recognise this song that has touched and united the souls of so many. I realise now that Angel Ariana has called upon on this beautiful song to play in the background to help calm me and clear my mind throughout my struggles. As the music continues to play, my angel turns to speak to me. Her eyes are lit up, her smile sparkling.

It is time.

As she stands straight and tall, her wings are spread out proud. I watch as the pool of light that circles around her feet begins to grow. It swirls around calmly to start with, growing larger and larger by the second. Suddenly I notice that it begins to steer itself off to the right of my guardian angel. As it grows and travels it illuminates the floor beneath us, lighting up part of the wall as well. The ground that was once dusty and lined with dirt now appears to be made out of a clean, white luxurious marble.

The pool of light has turned into a path. It continues to grow until it reaches the back of the wall that stands to my left. As the light moves up the wall, I can see that it is revealing something to me.

A wooden door rests in the wall. I am no longer blinded by the darkness of the room. No more do I struggle to see within my surroundings. I have been shown my way out.

I look at Angel Ariana and she nods to me. Absent of fear or anxiety, I place a bare foot onto the marble path. It is not cold as I had expected, but beautifully warm. The light guides me as I continue down the path.

I stop at the door. I reach my hand out and place it on the doorknob. I turn it, and open the door slightly. I must step through to my escape. My relief lies on the other side.

I turn round to face my angel. She smiles back reassuringly. Her wings are completely immersed in light now, each feather transparent, lit up by the love that comes straight from her heart. She nods to me again, encouraging me to step forward. I turn and face the door again. I know I must carry on. I can hear Angel Ariana speaking softly behind me.

Her words are whispered in harmony with the comforting instrumental of the song that still fills the air. I cross over the door to step into my release. As she continues to speak, the words of my angel guide me forward as I am shown the way out to my liberation.

Chapter Twenty Two

My dearest child, you have traveled through your life with strong courage, and for this you are greatly admired. Through your troubles you have succeeded in standing on the other side, knowing what is right. Your heart has been pure. However, your spirit has been overshadowed by that of another. It is now time for you to break free from his chains and move forward.

On earth, challenges are set in place to help the spirit grow and develop. In standing up to these difficulties you are assisting angels with our duties, meeting us in the middle as we work against man-made storms to maintain the motions of your realities.

The memories that remain within will always be there for you. It is important that you look to the scars of your battles so that you can help others as you progress along your journey. Throughout your own endeavors you will be required to call upon these memories from time to time and offer guidance to those who require it.

You are ready to cross over the bridge to a new course. You must not lose hope as you start along this path. You have built the strength within yourself to overcome the obstacles that lie ahead of you. You must believe in yourself and know in your heart that you are capable.

Walk on, and the angels will guide you. Have faith, and the light of the heavens with always be with you to show you the way. Walk on, keep your head held high, and remember:

You'll never walk alone.

Printed in Great Britain
by Amazon